WAITING

ON

FAITH

Tricia Cundiff

ISBN 978-1-7340359-2-6

This book is a work of fiction. Names, characters,
places, and incidents either are products of the
author's imagination or are used fictitiously. Any
resemblance to actual persons, living or dead, events,
or locales is entirely coincidental.

Tricia Cundiff
Visit my website at www.TriciaCundiff.com

Printed in the United States of America

First Printing: May 2020

For Lee
Always My Hero

Acknowledgments

The list grows of those that have figuratively walked with me through this book, helping me to add and take-away, explain and research, and, most of all, encourage.

Some of those–

Sissy (Betsy England), my aunt and so much more, motivator, support system, and often a shoulder to lean on,

Melanie Hunt Collins, my buddy since first grade, and the one that keeps me in line. Telling me like it is, and being the great teacher that she is, pushing me to excel – Mel, facing the years ahead with friends like you – it's going to be a blast!

Priscilla Poag Wanamaker, offering so much support with a kind reader's eye. Priscilla is a blessing who doesn't know the inspiration she gave to another student as I watched her on stage in high school, so confident and pretty, wearing that Panama hat with a purple hatband.   I wanted to have that confidence and fearlessness, and after so many years, I am working on it.

And, always,

Chad Lloyd, my son, and editor, my stack of finished and unfinished stories would be just that, a pile of stories. Without your encouragement and work, none of this could come to pass. Thank you, forever and forever, thank you. You are my light.

ONE
1974

P atch stood on the small bridge connecting the cottage to the shoreline. The waves were tumultuous now, with a storm out at sea. The lightning flashed in the distance highlighting the darkening sky as twilight descended on the island. Looking down at the ancient journal he held in his hands, he placed it in the old waterproof backpack he had used to protect it for years. This book, this story that brought him to this place right now, this was his marriage proposal. It wouldn't do to have the old leather and yellowed parchment damp. Passed down in his family for generations, dating back to the

1800s, this would be his way of asking for Lizzie's hand. The small ring he had managed to purchase was not magnificent enough for Lizzie, but it was all he could afford. The journal, though, he knew in his heart that it would be unique for Lizzie. She would understand.

Lizzie would love it here. Patch looked around, expecting her any moment. He had told her to meet him on the bridge. She would see it when she pulled up to the small cottage.

Patch smiled as he saw the Volkswagen Bug spray up gravel as it stopped suddenly. The young woman that opened the door wasn't exactly graceful as she crawled out of the low-riding car. Stretching and looking around, Lizzie saw him standing on the wooden walkway. The long black hair braided, as it seemed to be most of the time, swung back and forth as she ran. The young woman was slim, almost skinny, and could run like the wind. She had bested him several times around the track. The smile and deep brown eyes made his heart skip a beat as she hugged him tightly.

"I could hardly wait to get here! But the drive – oh, the drive was glorious! I have never driven that far by myself before. And I enjoyed it. I could sing as loud as I wanted, and no one complained!" She laughed and kissed him heartily on the mouth.

Pulling away after the warm kiss, Patch laughed with her and said, "Never, ever, will I tell you not to sing!"

"Sure, you say that now. You know I can't carry a tune, right?" She pulled at the strap of his backpack. "Going somewhere?"

"Okay, this is something I'll tell you about later. Can you walk down to the shore with me now? Or do you want to unload first?" He motioned towards her car.

"Oh no, we have got to go to this beach. You've bragged about it! Right now, buster." She started across the bridge, and Patch grabbed her hand. She looked back at him with a question in her eyes.

"We have to go together. My turn, remember? You took me to your mountain. You showed me the wonders of the Smokies. Now it's my turn to show you Sanibel." He put his arm around her shoulder.

"Patch, you're silly! I've been to the ocean before!" Lizzie looked at him and grinned.

Patch had become accustomed to his name. Brant Patrick Delamar did sound a little stuffy; he had to admit. Named after his mother's grandfather, he was proud of the name Brant, but he had become accustomed to the name Patch since early childhood.

Patch looked down at her with the sea winds whipping hair in her face and realized she could call him most anything she wanted as long as he could see the love in her eyes.

"Show me this beach that is so different than all the others!" Lizzie nuzzled under his arm as they crossed the bridge that took them over the tall seagrass to the sand. The lighthouse was visible as she looked to the south, and she could see the storm approaching from the east over the horizon.

Kicking off their sandals at the edge of the bridge, they entered the sand, Lizzie giggling as the soft powder made its way between her toes. The sky was darkening as the sun was setting behind them, yellow hues highlighting the cottage. A few stragglers were down the beach, making their way to shelter.

Lizzie looked down on the sand and saw the incredible array of shells, many of them moving with their sea creatures still living inside. "I've never seen so many shells on a beach!" she exclaimed.

"Yes, Sanibel does have its share. It's kind of silly to collect them down here if you live here. You can always go out and find some more. They are beautiful, aren't they?" Patch realized that he would see things anew through her. He watched as her eyes drew in the beauty of the surf, mighty and forceful, the tide showing its power. "We'll come back down and walk on the beach later, after the storm. It'll blow over quickly. They usually do."

"Usually? But not always, right?" Lizzie gazed out at the lightning.

"No, not always." Thunder was rolling overhead, but still far away. The colors of the sunset were magnificent, shining against the darkening clouds over the water. He realized that now, here was the time. He prayed, 'Lord, please let her say yes,' and gently turned her head towards his. "Lizzie?"

She looked at him puzzled, and then her eyes widened as he got down on one knee, sand blowing against his thighs. Carefully lying the backpack down on the sand, he reached in his pocket and pulled out the small box. Opening it, he pulled out the ring and reached for her hand.

Lizzie put one hand up to her mouth, then realized it was her ring hand. Smiling, with tears running down her face, she gave it to him.

"Elizabeth Oliver, I can't imagine any kind of happy life without you in it. I need you; I want you, I love you. If I could have Elvis singing in the background right now wearing his Hawaiian shirt, it couldn't be more perfect. God has blessed me with so much in my life, and He led me to you. I want to share everything with you. Our past, our present, and our future. Please be my Lizzie and marry me." He held the ring up with a question in his eyes.

Lizzie looked down at the man she loved with all her heart. "Yes, my Hero, dear Patch. I will always be your Lizzie if you'll always be my Patch."

Putting the ring on her finger, he stood and took her in his arms, kissing her deeply. Holding her close made him feel whole, complete. Answered prayers, he thought.

A large roll of thunder turned them towards the cottage. "We should go in before it starts raining. I could stand right here with you forever, but I do have something else for you," Patch said as he held up the backpack, "and I don't want it to get wet."

"Yes, and I want to meet your parents! Are they in the cottage?" Lizzie held tightly to his side, holding out her hand and admiring the sparkle the small diamond displayed. "Are they happy about this?"

Patch smiled down at her, nodding. "Mom will be back soon. She had a meeting at church. Mom is so excited about meeting you – she's just mad that it has taken so long! Dad is looking forward to meeting you, too, but he's on a trip with the youth at church. He'll be back in a couple of days."

A few minutes later, car unloaded, Lizzie was walking through the small cottage, exclaiming about the wall covered with bookshelves and the view of the dunes and seagrass. No drapes adorned these windows; there was no one to see from the oceanside.

"We don't walk around in here without robes in the morning. Occasionally we'll have someone walk up from the beach, but they don't usually come up to the cottage. It's pretty clear someone lives here." Patch walked over to the window and looked out. "I like waking up in the morning and looking out at the shades of red and orange as the sun comes up. Mom says something now and again about putting up some kind of curtain or shade, but I love it open. I want to see it. Having shutters in the bedrooms is enough. There are shutters on the outside, for high winds and hurricanes. But so far, we haven't lost anything important."

"I can see why you like the view," Lizzie said as she came up beside him and put her hand into his. "Your Sanibel is beautiful. I can't wait to see more of it. Especially now, that I'm going to be a real islander, at least part-time!" She held up her hand and splayed her fingers in his face, showing off her ring.

Patch pulled her back to the couch, facing the windows. "Sit, please. Let me tell you about this," he said as he placed the journal between them.

Lizzie couldn't stop smiling and looking at her finger, adorned with her engagement ring. Patch touched her chin and turned her eyes to his. "Be serious, now, please?" he said with a smile.

"All serious," Lizzie said, deliberately placing a frown on her face and putting her hand under her leg. "I'll just put it away and not be all girly-girl."

Not sure if she would stay solemn for very long, Patch jumped in. "You remember I told you about this cottage, well, not this exact one. I told you once about my great, great something, grandmother. Her name was Maddie?"

"Yes, but not so much. You said something like 'it was a long story.' I do remember questioning you about it, and you said 'all in time' so mysteriously. This was like two hundred years ago, right? When she was alive?" Lizzie, dropping the teasing tone, looked at him quizzically.

"I do know a lot about her. From this." He held it out to her.

Lizzie took it gently. "It's very old," she said, turning it over. As she started to untie the thin rope, Patch put his hands over hers.

"Lizzie," Patch said, "this journal has been passed down in my family from generation to generation, beginning with Maddie's son, Joseph. Joseph gave it to his only daughter, Isabella. It belongs to my family, and you are my family. It is yours. It is yours to give to one of our children. My father gave it to my mother; my mother gave it to me. I want you to read it whenever you want. And I would love to talk to you about it, although I can add little to its contents."

Untying the faded and frayed rope that held the journal closed, she opened to the first page. Words Patch knew well, written in the lopsided hand he recognized as Maddie's writing, he followed along with Lizzie as she read from the opening page. A date was in the corner, 'April 1818.'

April 1818

'I leave now for this New World, the Americas. Padre has promised me this last trip before I am to be wed, and I intend to make the most of it. Since I am now old, and Padre has assured me I must marry now or forever be a single old lady, I suppose I have no choice. I must be very plain, indeed, to be wed to such an old man. My mother, a very proper Englishwoman, tells me I am beautiful, but my mirror tells me something different. With a Spaniard for a father and the beauty he married from England, I should have some sort of looks about me. But no. Evidently, I inherited the worst of the lineage from both. And I am sick to death of being told to mind my place! Too full of airs for the likes of suitable suitors? Pshaw!

I will record everything wonderful that is sure to happen on this voyage, and in my visit to this new place they are making so much ado about. As my first entry into this beautiful new journal my Mama has gifted me for this my fifteenth birthday, I shall always remember the trunks going up the ramp onto the ship amid the yelling of the men making way to set sail. I have friends on board, this being a trip for families yearning to see the new land about which there is such a ruckus. My Padre has settled me into a cabin with another young woman, Victoria, not much older than I. She is English, so it is well that I have studied the language and can converse with her. Her father and mother have a cabin next door to ours, and they will be my guardians on this voyage. Padre and Mama could not get away, and truth be told, I am glad. I am set to be adventurous on this trip and to elude my guardians whenever possible. Why should I worry about consequence, when I have nothing to look forward to when I return to Spain?'

Lizzie, head bowed as she read, carefully held the old leather that bound the fragile pages together. Raising her eyes to his, tears streaming down her face, she smiled. The brilliance of that smile had won Patch's heart forever; it beat stronger for her with each echo of that smile. Quietly, she spoke. "This is a story of wonder. This girl – only fifteen! – that became your, your – greats–again grandmother! I cannot wait to read it all, to know how it came to be. And here, you told me, this happened on Sanibel?"

Patch nodded. Taking the book and closing it, tying it loosely, he said, "You can read all you want, but I know you must be tired."

"I'll take it to bed with me if you don't mind. I promise I will take very good care of it," looking up at Patch as he smiled at her. "I have never received such a wonderful gift."

Neither of them had heard Patch's mom enter. She stayed out of sight, listening at the door to the intimate conversation between her son and her future daughter-in-law. Her eyes also filling with tears, she looked up and voiced a silent 'thank you, God.'

TWO

Patch awakened to the sound of his mother rattling around in the kitchen. The smell of coffee swept through the room. Turning over to look at the time, he saw he had missed the sunrise. There would be others.

Walking into the kitchen a few minutes later, he kissed his mom on the forehead, looking down at her graying hair pulled back into a ponytail. "Hey, mom. I'll have some of that coffee. Maybe take Lizzie down to the beach for a walk when she gets up."

"She's already down there, I think," his mother said as she poured a cup and placed it in front of him. "I heard the door close earlier, and her room is empty." Sheila Delamar poured another cup and handed it to her son. "Why don't you take her a cup, too?"

"I think I will," Patch said, taking the cup. He looked at his mother, a question in his eyes.

"She's perfect," his mother said, brushing her hand through his hair, long and hanging down in his eyes. She didn't understand these styles.

Patch's mom and future wife met when Sheila showed Lizzie to her bedroom and the closet with blankets and towels. Hugging her tightly, she had briefly welcomed her into the cottage with happy tears when Lizzie showed her the ring.

Sheila Delamar watched from the window as her son walked to the bridge that would take him over the seagrass to Lizzie. Hugging her elbows, Sheila wished her husband was there with her. He would be home tomorrow, thank goodness. He would love his son's choice, she knew. They had prayed for this. God had answered their prayer for the person to share their son's life, to be by his side through this roller coaster ride. Smiling to herself, she looked up and said, "Yeah, I know. They'll mess up, but You'll put them back where they're supposed to be. We did our share of messing up, and You were always there to pick us up. Thank You." She looked back out the window as memories pushed in.

Patch had wandered away from his life here on the island, but he had returned. Sheila sat down at the counter and pulled an old photograph album over. She had pulled it out first thing this morning, ready to show Lizzie all the old pictures they had of Patch. Flipping through the pages, Patch at the beach, playing in the water. Patch watching as the turtles made their way to the ocean after hatching from eggs. The three of them in front of the cottage before they had the porch added. Who made that picture? She couldn't remember.

Patch in the old Jeep, heading off to college. The back entirely loaded, Patch was smiling and waving as he pulled away, long hair blowing. He laughingly told them, 'Sure I'm a hippie, but I'm a drug-free hippie! I promise!" Why so far to Tennessee to go to college, she didn't understand. Neither did Nolan, but he said to let him go. Even after they found the marijuana stashed in his bedroom, Nolan threw it out and shook his head. "We have to trust him, Sheila. And we have to trust God." MTSU in Tennessee had one of the best mass media programs available, and that's what he wanted. A friend he met over the summer between his junior and senior year convinced him to come and share a dorm room.

Time had proven Nolan correct. Patch may have strayed, but God brought him back. The first couple of years away had been troublesome, and Sheila knew that her knees had calluses on them from the constant praying. Then Patch met Lizzie. A broken-down car had stopped them going to some concert they wanted to attend. Woodstock. Something happened that weekend. Sheila didn't know what, but Patch was different after that. She shivered, not wanting to remember the two years he was gone.

It was all okay now. Patch had a respectable job, working for a radio station in Nashville. He was hoping to work with a national company that worked with Christian broadcasting eventually, but was happy with his current 'gig.' Lizzie was doing her student teaching in a small community outside of Nashville, and loved it, Patch said.

Yes, God is good, Sheila thought. Smiling, she looked up in the air and shook her head. "I know it's of no use, but I do have to worry, you know." I'm sure that God shakes His head in exasperation with me many times, she thought.

Patch saw Lizzie sitting in the sand with her toes buried in the sand. The ripples of water from small waves tickled her feet, but she didn't seem to notice. He sat down in the sand next to her but didn't speak. She was quiet. Looking over at her, he could see tear tracks on her face.

"Lizzie?"

Lizzie shook her head, not trusting herself to speak. She put her head down and pulled her knees up to her chest. Sand and wind whipping at her hair, Patch wanted to hold her but knew her too well to allow himself that comfort. He could wait.

Finally, she broke the silence between them. "I can't," she said softly. He was barely able to hear her over the sound of the waves crashing against the sand.

Patch sighed. He had prayed and hoped that she would see more clearly now, but the evil was intense. He sat there with her. He could wait.

THREE
1968

The first time he saw her, in the fall of 1968, he considered her a hothead. Didn't she know that the college campus was not the place to make enemies? The enemies were out there, the government, the establishment. Probably another freshman, really just wanting to cry and go home to mommy and daddy.

Patch watched as the two girls argued over a textbook in the college bookstore. The last one on the shelf, a man was trying to tell them there were probably others at the bookstore off-campus. The shorter of the two, and to Patch's way of thinking, the prettiest although she was also the loudest, heaved a disgusted sigh and let go of the book. Turning around, she headed towards the front of the store. Patch followed, interested, but not quite sure why.

He stepped out the door, looking right and left but didn't see her. She couldn't have gotten too far. Then he spotted her on the sidewalk, riding a bike. A bike. He didn't know anyone that had a bike up here nowadays. Shaking his head, bewildered at his interest, he returned to the bookstore. He needed one more book to finish out his list. Two more years, he thought. Then on to the biggest radio station that would have him. If he didn't go to 'Nam.

It wasn't the last time that day he spotted Lizzie. As luck, or God intervening he would think later, would have it, she stepped out from nowhere in front of him and they collided. Almost falling over into the rack where she had parked her bike, he righted her by her shoulders and said, "Watch it there, Sheba!"

"What?" the girl said, looking at him curiously. "What did you call me?"

"Oh, sorry. My dad, my dad calls my mom that sometimes. Says she's beautiful like Bathsheba. And her name is Sheila, so, uh, sorry. It just slipped out." Now embarrassed, Patch looked away from the most amazing eyes he had ever seen, the golden streaks surrounding the honey-brown iris. The darkest brown hair, almost black. Bathsheba fit.

The incredible girl in front of him pulled at his sleeve, pulling his gaze back down to hers. "I'm Elizabeth. Most people call me Lizzie, but Sheba is okay, too." She grinned up at him. "I need a friend today. How about it? Want to grab a coke?"

Patch looked at her and smiled. "I'm Patch. Sure, I have time to be a friend today, and at a better place than here. There's a little five and dime with a lunch counter and booths. It's next to the bookstore off-campus. You need to go there, right?"

"Not only tall and good-looking, but you're a mind reader, too? I'm a lucky girl!" She was laughing at him.

Patch looked at her quizzically. He didn't think of himself as good-looking. His dark brown hair had streaks of lighter shades from the sun, and his eyes were green. He was tall, he guessed, at six feet, he towered over some. Looking in the mirror in the morning, he didn't see anything special. Not everyone could have Presley's looks, and no matter how hard he tried, he couldn't get the lopsided grin down, either. But hey, if she thought he was good-looking, he was happy with that.

"I overheard you in the campus bookstore. You gave in pretty quickly to that other girl. Scared?" He hoped he sounded casual, not too interested. He didn't want to scare her off, not now. Not ever. There was something here that held him bound to her voice.

"Scared? Nope. Not scared, just tired." Her face changed, a little sad. "I just didn't want to fight about it."

Wanting to see that smile again, Patch sputtered. "Well, come on, let's try out that other bookstore."

"My bike?" she said, looking back at the rack.

"Oh yeah. Well, can we take it to your dorm room? Is that where you keep it?" He thought himself brilliant. What an excellent way to find out where she was rooming!

Lizzie smiled again and lit up his world. "Okay, yeah. It's just around the corner. I'm in Rutledge Hall. Ground floor, thankfully. I expected to see lots of these here, but so far, I'm the only one. Why does everyone want to walk everywhere?"

"The campus isn't that big, you know. Middle Tennessee is pretty small compared to the big universities. You can walk around the whole thing pretty quickly. But someday, this place will be one of the biggest in Tennessee, I bet." Patch took her bike from the rack and walked with her to her dorm.

The afternoon turned into early evening, and when Patch walked her back to her dorm before curfew, they were both laughing. They had stopped for a few minutes at a protest that never quite got enough people to be called anything other than a light gathering. Deciding that the protesters weren't sure what they were protesting, they walked away, trying to keep from laughing out loud.

Stopping at the steps to the dorm, Lizzie turned and grinned up at him. "Thank you."

Patch looked at her and furrowed his eyebrows. "What for?"

"You did it. I needed a friend, and you were one. This could have been a pretty yuck day, but it wasn't. That's why." Lizzie turned and ran up the steps. As she opened the big double doors that no boy was allowed to cross, he yelled up and stopped her.

"What about tomorrow?"

"Oh, I'll be okay tomorrow, I think." She smiled at him, nodded, and went inside.

Patch would see her tomorrow, or at least the next day. He would make sure of it. He knew where she lived, and he knew some of her classes. He had learned quite a lot. They had talked for hours.

Lizzie had told him about her family, an older brother who lived in Canada, and her favorite place in the mountains. "A hillbilly?" he had teased her, and she smacked him on the arm, but not too hard. He told her about the island and how he loved the ocean. They talked about school and the classes they were taking. He was right; she was a freshman and thought she wanted to be a teacher, but wasn't sure. He was two years older, a junior, and knew exactly what he wanted. Majoring in journalism, and taking some low-level engineering classes, he wanted to be in radio. Somewhere on the radio. It would be great to be a disc jockey, but he would be happy to be working in the station on the boards. Music, this great new music, he wanted to be a part of it. Nashville wasn't exactly the kind of music he craved, but he had a hunch that someday country music would be a little more upbeat. Roger Miller and Johnny Cash were mixing it up some. They even talked about his childhood dream of being an astronaut. Growing up on an island where you could see the rockets taking off from Canaveral once they were high enough was an inspiration for all boys in the area.

They talked a long time, over Cokes, and then grilled cheese sandwiches. Patch lay in bed, remembering every moment. Staring at the ceiling, he realized that they didn't talk about anything personal. He sat up in bed, thinking about the conversation. He asked about her high school, her friends, her church. She always changed the subject, back to something trivial. There was more he wanted to know. She was an enigma, a mystery he wanted to solve. She was...she was...wow. He was a broadcast journalism major and couldn't find the word he wanted. He smiled at himself. Maybe because it was Lizzie. There were no words.

FOUR
1974

Remembering that first meeting and realizing how far they had come, Patch smiled to himself. Lizzie was unsure of herself, but she would find her way. She accused him of jumping too quickly sometimes, but this was not one of those times. He had put a lot of thought into this, in asking her to marry him.

Lizzie was still sitting there quietly, staring out into the ocean when a large red-coated dog barked and jumped towards them. A man was holding a leash, although not tight enough, it seemed. She calmed as she saw Patch laughing as the dog licked him across the face.

"Sorry about that, boy. Your mom said you two were down here, and I thought I'd give Lady here a quick walk on the beach. She's been with me for two days, and misses the water." A bear of a man smiled down at the two of them as the dog, Lady, took off for the water to retrieve a mostly flat football the man had thrown.

Lizzie held her hand over her eyes to block out the sun. Standing in front of her was Patch, only heavier and older. Dark hair sprinkled with gray, a silvery beard just beginning to need a trim. Ruddy complexion that had seen plenty of sunshine, but didn't appear any the worse for it. The great smile was Patch, all Patch. A hearty laugh, she thought. Nothing held back.

"You must be Elizabeth. Our boy here is quite under your spell, I believe. My name's Nolan, Nolan Delamar." He held out his hand, smiling down at her, perhaps not realizing that he had interrupted her pain. Patch wasn't sure she would respond.

Lizzie stood and clasped his hand, smiling a sad smile. "Hello, Mr. Delamar. I am so honored to meet you. I'm sorry, I'm not myself right now." She looked down at her feet when Patch's father looked at her curiously.

"You look breath-taking to me, Elizabeth. I can see why Patch is so taken with you," he said as he let her hand go. "I didn't want to disturb you two, both of you so deep in thought. Do you mind if I sit down?"

"Of course not, Mr. Delamar. And please, call me Lizzie."

"Lizzie, it is. Patch, would you mind throwing the ball with Lady a few times? I hate to say it, but she has worn me out!" Nolan Delamar settled himself on the sandy beach as he had done thousands of times before, and handed the mangled football to Patch. Lady switched from jumping on Nolan Delamar to lunging at the football held by Patch.

Patch stood and smiled down at his father. "Don't be hard on her, Dad; she just got here!" A little concerned for Lizzie, but knowing that his father had great instincts, he ran down to the water with Lady.

"I interrupted something mighty personal, didn't I, Lizzie? I'm so sorry," Nolan's voice was inquiring, but not exceptionally so.

"I think I've hurt your son," Lizzie responded, surprised at herself for speaking so honestly.

"Maybe, but he's tough. Is it reversible? Can you fix the hurt?" Nolan asked softly.

"I think maybe I have to be fixed myself. And I'm not sure I can be fixed."

Nolan looked over at the young girl sitting on the sand beside him, the love of his son's life. Patch had told him so. He could see the pain in her eyes through the tears rolling down her cheek. He leaned back, elbows resting on the sand. Letting out a long breath, he spoke softly.

"Everybody's fixable; I have to believe that on some level. God works miracles every day. And He can fix anything and anybody. I think you just have to believe it and trust Him to show the way."

Lizzie looked over at him. "You sound just like Patch."

"I'm not an exceptionally smart man, Elizabeth, excuse me, Lizzie," he said when she started to interrupt. "But all I have to do is look around, look around really good. I know that God did all of this." His gaze went to Patch and Lady at the edge of the water. "Patch is a brilliant man. I guess he got it from his mother," he said, laughing lightly. "But I am happy to hear that he has talked about God, that college didn't take his faith away from him. He's always been upfront about what he thinks about God and Jesus. Some don't agree, but he won't back down. He's right about that. Me, too. God is God, and God is good. He can fix everything and everybody."

"Maybe He can. Maybe He just doesn't want to fix me. Maybe I'm too damaged and not worth fixing," Lizzie mumbled.

Nolan took Lizzie's chin in his fingers and turned it toward him. "My Patch loves you very much; you are his 'soul-mate' he told me. That's what you kids say now, right? He would do anything for you. So you're worth it, never forget it. But God? God loves you more than anyone else possibly can because He's God! Perfect. Perfect Love. For you, Lizzie. Trust that, if nothing else." He stood up and brushed the sand from his clothes. "Okay, 'nuf preaching for today. Sorry, Lizzie, I get a little carried away sometimes! Why don't I go get Lady and let you and your Patch have some time alone?"

Watching Patch's father walk down to the water's edge and pat his son on the back, Lizzie took a deep breath. 'Oh, God,' she thought. 'I want to believe it. I want to believe it every time, and then I bring it all back again. I can't let it go. Is it because I'm not supposed to?'

Patch sat down on the sand beside her and laid his hand out, palm up, between them. She placed her hand in his. He squeezed her hand and brought it up to his lips. Kissing the fingers, he closed his eyes, not speaking.

"I want to be with you always. I want us to be happy. But..." Lizzie hesitated

Patch looked at her face; uncertainty painted in her eyes. He grasped her hand tight and smiled. "I want to be with you always, too. And we will be happy, but not always. There will be times when we'll be angry or sad or just plain bored, I think. Although I can't think of any time I would be bored if I was with you. But after, I don't know, seventy or eighty years together; there might be a time when you'll be bored with me. That's okay. I love you, and I know that you love me. It's okay if I bore you, I think. Because by that time, you'll know my heart and soul as I'll know yours. I want to spend all of these years doing just that. Getting to know you, heart and soul."

Lizzie giggled, she couldn't help it. "Heart and Soul? Really, you're going with that song?" She knew she was leaping from one emotion to the other, but couldn't help it.

"Now that you mention it, yes, that's what I want playing at our wedding," Patch said as he put his arm around her.

"We'll see." Lizzie looked over at him with pain in her eyes but a smile on her lips. She looked down at the ring on her finger. "I'm not sure we should be engaged. I'm not sure about anything. And the book, the journal. Something so precious to your family. I'm not sure I can, that I, well, that I deserve anything like that. What if..."

"What if? Lizzie, there's no what if. It's you and me. Aren't you sure about me?" Patch questioned.

"I love you, that I know," Lizzie answered as she raised her lips to his.

Kissing her softly, Patch prayed silently, 'Let me say the right things, Lord, let me help her.'

Lizzie started to speak again, but Patch put a finger on her lips. "Wait, me first," he began. "You're going to be here for a few days. We're going to explore this island. I want to show you so much! Maybe I'm moving too fast, but you know what? I'll wait for you to catch up. You and me, kiddo. It'll always be you and me."

Lizzie looked at the love in Patch's eyes and knew she couldn't say no. She probably should get in her car and go home, but she couldn't. If God was around, maybe He wanted her to stay. Please, God, help me, she thought to herself. She nodded at Patch and put her arms around his neck. "I don't know why you wait on me. After all you've been through, why do you think I'm worth it?" she said into his shoulder.

"You are my heart. You waited on me, for two long years, you waited on me. The only things that kept me going were your letters and knowing you were waiting. I will wait for you, as long as you need." Patch kissed the top of her head and closed his eyes in thankful prayer.

FIVE

May 10, 1818

The first two weeks were difficult, to say very little about it. I was sickened by the motion of the ship at first, but became accustomed to the rise and fall quite quickly. However, my cabin mate did not do the same. While many aboard, besides the crew and I, are staying in their quarters, I find myself on top much of the time, out of desire to avoid the constant hacking and smells below decks. There is one other, a Master Jamison, that walks with me in the morning air. Having found out that he is to be married to my cabin mate, we have become friends. He asks about her constantly, and I assure him that she is being cared for, but cannot stand up without becoming violently ill. They are in love; it is clear. He is a right handsome hombre, although not entirely to my liking. Of course, the old gent I am to marry is not to my taste at all, but I fear I have no way out of it.

May 24, 1818

I have begun to think I will never set foot on land again. We are two weeks past our date of arrival at the island, which name evades me at present. We were to stop there before we headed around the cap of the land known as Florida to visit cities along the great river that continues to haunt Napoleon. It has been said that he regrets decisions he made as to the route that runs deep into the Americas. Little I know of these events, and I don't want to bother myself with them. A storm, which put everyone back to bed after scarcely a week on calm waters, has put us off our course. Even my friend, Master Jamison, has taken to his bed.

"I'm anxious to read more," Lizzie told Patch at dinner that night. "I'm still in the middle of the voyage and haven't got to the part where they come here to the island. Do you mind if I beg off after one game?"

Sheila and Nolan Delamar asked that they play Scrabble after dinner and before a walk on the beach. The weather was clear now, and Patch wanted to show Lizzie the magic of the beach after dark.

"Okay, one game and a short walk after dark. Mom, I'll clean up the kitchen after we get back, and Lizzie locks herself in her room to read. You and Dad need to catch up since he's returned" Patch looked over at Lizzie and smiled. She looked happier.

Nolan Delamar looked over at his wife and nodded. "It's a deal, boy. Why don't you and Lizzie take Lady with you to the beach while your mom and I take a bike ride down to the lighthouse?"

"In the dark?" Patch asked.

"We know our way around. Besides, there's plenty of light from that big moon out there," his father said as he held out his hand to his mother, Sheila.

Taking his hand, she stood and kissed his cheek. "I'll be right back, going to get my tennis shoes."

A short while later, Nolan and Sheila Delamar made their way across the graveled path to the lighthouse on the end of the island. Their bikes parked in the racks provided by the park service, Nolan's flashlight in hand, they walked hand in hand marveling at the sounds only a place far removed from the bustle of busy streets and noisy establishments can attain. The only sounds were those of the rustling of bushes and trees as birds flitted from one branch to another. The laps of the waves hitting the rocks at the end of the water. Insects barely chirping, lest they destroy the golden silence. An occasional voice and laughter, but very soft as if the others walking the beach also did not want to disturb the magnitude of silent reflection.

Helping his wife to sit down on a large rock positioned to look out past the lighthouse to the water, Nolan stared up at the rotating light above. "It's so good to be back home," he said quietly, so only Sheila could hear. "I'm thankful that the island kings in their great wisdom have ruled that outside lights should be out by 9:00 and that we would not have all the big hotels and such here in our piece of paradise."

"Some people like all that stuff, you know," Sheila said, kidding him as she took his hand in hers.

"They can have it. This is it for me." Looking up at the stars, he continued, "I like Lizzie. I think she really loves our boy. But I'm not sure about something."

"Yeah, I know. Elizabeth is upset about something, hiding something deep inside. I don't want her pain to become our son's pain." Sheila crossed her arms together and shivered, not from the cold.

Nolan nodded, "I know. There's a darkness in her, in Lizzie. I don't know what it is. Oh, I don't mean that she's evil," he said as he saw the questioning look on Sheila's face. "Just that there's a darkness inside that she can't let out or something."

Sheila sat there quietly for a few minutes before she spoke. "I think you recognize that darkness because Patch had that darkness inside of him when he came back. I was scared that he would never find his way out of the dark."

Nolan let out a deep sigh. "You're right. But he found his way. With God's help, he found his way. Vietnam messed up a lot of kids, Sheila. We're one of the lucky ones. We got our son back, and he's whole again." He stopped and looked over at his wife. "I was worried about losing you, too, you know. When we didn't know where Patch was, if he was dead or alive those last six months he was gone, I thought I was going to lose you, too."

Sheila took a deep breath. "I felt dead inside. I was afraid to feel anything. I just had to keep praying, praying over and over. At the same time, I knew that there were lots of mothers and fathers out there praying, too. And yet, prayers were not answered. God didn't say yes to some of those mothers and daddies out there! I was so scared that I wouldn't get him back," Sheila felt the old emotions rising in her, the fear and anguish.

"I knew that you were hurting, too. I just didn't have anything to give. I'm so sorry, Nolan. You were there for me, and I wasn't there for you," Sheila looked up into the eyes of the man that she had been with for her entire adult life.

"Sheila, my love. You were there; we held each other when we cried. We prayed together; we begged God together; we yelled at God together. Our souls were united in our grief, our pain, our search for answers. As it should be. As God would have it to be. And Patch came home. Remember when we got the phone call? He was coming home? We didn't know if he was dead or alive, but they said he was coming home. I could hear you on the phone, even though you were barely speaking above a whisper, and you asked how he was coming home? I knew what you were asking. Was he coming in a casket? But he wasn't, and when I saw that tear fall from your eyes and the smile on your face, my heart filled with joy that our son was coming home, and my wife would survive." Nolan looked down at the ground, remembering the raw emotions.

"When he walked through that door from the plane, I felt as if I could breathe again. Like I had been holding my breath until he was here. My heart could start beating again. I saw the pain in his eyes, the sadness in the way he held himself, and I hurt for him. But a part of my heart was singing that he was home again." Sheila stared out at the moonlit ocean and laughed softly. "We sure do get off the beaten path, don't we? We were talking about Lizzie, about Lizzie and Patch."

"I believe that Patch is the one that can pull that darkness out. She is good for our boy. Did you know that she begged him to go to Canada when he received his draft notice? But when he didn't, she waited. I'm sure her agony during his absence was difficult, too. And then even when he came back, he didn't go to her for weeks. That had to have been miserable for her. And we didn't know. I'm still not sure why he didn't want us to know how deep their relationship had become."

Sheila shook her head. "No, I don't know that either. Did he ever talk to you, ever even mention what went on over there? In Vietnam?" She sighed when Nolan shook his head. "I was hoping that Patch could talk to you about it. He said he couldn't talk to me about it; Patch said he didn't know if he would ever be able to talk to anyone."

"He just let me in on bits and pieces. I know it was terrible. His lieutenant was killed, and he had to step up. I think that preyed upon him. He was in charge of these boys and didn't know what he was leading them into. He was the same age as most of them, and only older than the rest by a couple of years. He continued to lead them in the same direction, but it was a trap. His unit was either killed or captured, and because he was in charge, he got the worst of the interrogations. He left Vietnam with seven of the fifteen that were in his unit after the marines came and overpowered the camp where they were being held. From what I've been able to find out, Patch was the reason the seven survived. If he hadn't taken the brunt of the abuse from their captors, it's likely more of them would not have made it."

"When did you learn all of this? It's the first I've heard about it," Sheila asked, confused that Nolan had not told her before.

"I have a letter in my briefcase back at the house. I'll let you read it. It's from the family of one of the boys that did come back with Patch. And I have a letter for Patch, too, from the boy. I picked up the mail on my way out of town last week and didn't want to talk about it over the phone. Now, my darling wife," he reached over and pulled her closer to him, "is the first time I've had you alone long enough to talk about anything!"

"And I'm so glad you're home," Sheila said as she raised her lips to his wonderfully familiar kiss.

SIX

July 1818

There is much to write. I have only received my journal back this day, and I am not sure which day it is. Our belongings, after being rifled through by these miscreants, were thrown into a pile. At the very least, I found my satchel with my journal, and may God bless her, my mother's Bible, given to me on the day I left Spain. I fear what I write will never be read or shared by me with my children and my children's children, as I once thought.

I know that I have been in this sordid place for a few weeks, so I think it must be at the very least, July. Pirates overtook our ship. A horrible, horrible moment in time. I cannot explain the terrible way we were treated, and indeed, we have lost the men from our ship. Some, I fear, to the depth of the ocean, and I lost sight of where they took the others. I watched as Master Jamison was pushed aside as he was trying to protect Victoria from the wandering hands of the pirates who boarded our ship. I don't know what became of most of the ships' passengers and crew; I fear they are lost. Only the young women, as well as some of the older ones, were carried aboard the pirate's ship and taken away. I was trying to comfort Victoria as well as looking for her parents when I was pushed and shoved toward the boards that linked the two ships. Almost falling off the planks, a most evil-looking man pulled me up and motioned me towards the filthy arms of another pirate, waiting to take me on board.

I have not seen Victoria again, although I have not been able to look everywhere. We have not been beaten or raped, but are treated horribly. Not being able to bathe was the worst of the maladies that surrounded us here, but that was somewhat remedied in the past few days. Two men began bringing large vats of warm water, and we have taken turns to clean ourselves.

We are on land. At least that is something. The pirates dropped anchor offshore this desolate-

looking place and ferried us over in small rowing boats. There are a few of the rank-smelling varmints here watching over us, but the ship has left and not returned. We are required to fix food from the fish and small animals they bring us, as well as some types of vegetables they bring in. I don't know where they get it. The young women I have met have few, if any, cooking skills, and we have had to learn quickly what works and what doesn't. Many of them spend most of their time crying and wailing, and it is rapidly getting on my nerves. I am trying to be consoling and helpful, but my fear and anger overcome the more genteel qualities I should have as a young lady.

There are several buildings here, most of them housing women. There are smaller buildings around a central cabin that appears to house the captain of the pirates, where he holds his meetings with his underlings, I suppose. Not being able to get an exact count, I estimate that there are between 60 to possibly 80 or more women, and at least 25 pirates. Our ship is not the only one that has been captured. The pirates keep a close eye on the buildings and don't respond to any query.

Any attempts to talk to any of these foul-smelling men are met with sneers and remarks not bearing writing down. It is apparent that they have been instructed, however, to leave us alone and not force themselves upon us. At least it is evident in the section of the makeshift hut where I reside. I have heard loud laughing and yelps coming from other places. From the ridiculous female giggles, there is probable evidence that inappropriate attachments are transpiring.

None of us know where we are; therefore, we are hesitant to try to escape. Indeed, I haven't talked to anyone that would even contemplate the idea. But I can't stop thinking about it myself. The ship will come back. I do not doubt that it will not bring good news. It will be another few weeks before anyone will think to look for us, and I'm quite sure that we are not in a location that would be easy to find.

Lizzie carefully closed the old journal and set the book on the small nightstand beside her bed. Leaning back against the pillows she had propped up, she stared up at the ceiling. She wanted to read much more, but she was exhausted. Magdalena, the name written in the front cover. Such a beautiful name. This is the Maddie that Patch had mentioned before, but when she asked that he tell more, he had been mysterious. He had always said 'someday, maybe,' and then changed the subject. The last time she heard him say her name had been in church. It struck her as very odd that while everyone else was praying, she heard him say very quietly under his breath, 'you were right, Maddie.' But when she questioned him about it later, he just looked at her and smiled.

"You'll get it later," he replied with a mischievous grin. She had swatted at him but had allowed him to change the subject, as always.

She took a deep breath. Something in these pages helped Patch, gave him direction, and helped him when he was at his lowest. She knew that. If only Maddie could show her some guidance, too. Having only just begun reading the journal, Lizzie already realized that Maddie was an exceptional person and a young girl in a terrifying situation. What had Patch said? Something was tickling the back of her memory, something about the most horrible...yes, when everything is at the most frightful you can think of, look for God. His miracle is ready for you to grab. Maddie prayed; Maddie believed. You could see that from the journal. Did her trust in God bring her through? Was it because she believed that she survived?

I believe, I do! Well, maybe not like Patch, but I believe. God's around, sure, He's everywhere. And He probably helped Maddie out of a lot of bad situations. After all, she was a pretty good person, right? She deserved it.

I can't think about this anymore. Sleep is what I need. I'll read more tomorrow. And think more tomorrow. And look at my love more tomorrow. Oh, Patch, I do want us to work. I want us to make it. God, if you are there and listening to me, me? I love him; I love Patch. I love his family. I love it here. I love Your world. Help me to believe. Really, really believe.

SEVEN

Patch, just a day. Do something with your mom and dad, relax, forget I'm here! I just want one day, all day by myself. I'll probably read the entire day!" Lizzie looked up into eyes with her nose wrinkled up, begging. He couldn't deny her.

"Okay, a full day. But I ..."

"No!" she interrupted him. "I know what you are going to say. There's so much to see and do while I'm here. But I'll be back, right? At least, I'll probably be back," she looked up at him and saw his face fall. "I'll be back. I need to do this. I need to read all of Maddie's story before we talk about anything. I want to see Sanibel through her eyes."

Patch understood. And maybe she was right. He had envisioned her reading a little and then having the chance for the two of them to talk about it before she read more. But if he genuinely wanted Maddie's words to mean something to Lizzie, it was probably the right thing to do. Read the entire journal.

"It's not a short story," Patch began, "and it takes you on some twists and turns."

"I know," Lizzie said. "It's okay, I'm a fast reader, and I read even faster when it's something I like. And I like it. I truly do like it. And because it's your grandmother great-something, I like it even more."

Thankful that Patch had agreed to give her a day and not disturb her, Lizzie prepared a glass of iced tea. Patch and his parents had left to go to the mainland for some shopping and promised that they wouldn't return until late, probably after sunset. Her only responsibility was to walk Lady. She would enjoy that. Lady was a special dog.

Curling up on the couch, iced tea on the side table and Lady curled up on the other end. Lizzie looked out the window. A slight breeze was blowing. Appropriate, she thought, as she opened the journal to the next entry.

August 1818

We are on an island. All these women, these pirates, these horrid huts, some quite odd animals and alligators. I tried to find my way, hopefully to someone that would help. Leaving at first dawn one morning, I tiptoed gently out of the clearing, not worried that I would wake the pirates, but not wanting to disturb the young women from their much-needed sleep, restless though it was. Their fright might have awakened the men I wanted to avoid. I was gone for three, maybe four days. I can't quite keep it straight.

There is little on this island other than these pirates. I thought I saw someone early one morning as I rose from my hiding place between two trees, but they were quick to run, and I may have imagined it, coming out of a dream. Very little to eat also. Some berries, but they made me very sick. I did find water, a small stream most certainly closer to the middle of the island, but it was foul-smelling. I had to drink anyway but tried to take tiny sips. There was no salt in the taste, but earthy just the same. And of course, the alligator. A small one or I might not be here to record my adventure, such as it was.

As I followed the stream, it became broader and deeper and evidently, more to the liking of the monster itself. I certainly didn't want to stay in the water to meet the parents of this angry animal. Do parents of alligators follow their little ones? I will have to ask someone that someday if there is ever anyone that I come in contact with that would have any knowledge of something so obscure. I am rambling, I am aware. But to be able to sit and write, and not be so very hungry and thirsty. I was quite deliberate in my trampling through the jungle of trees to keep the sun in front of me, lest I lose my way. But then, the ocean again. And land far away, over the horizon. I will not try an escape again. Well, at least not without a better plan. Perhaps a boat will show up, and I can take it? I've never sailed a boat, but how hard could it be, after all? There's a sail, and then you row. If it is a little one, a small sail. I have seen little boats in the water, canoes, I think. They are rowing them back and forth to the big ship but without the benefit of a sail.

Yes, the pirates are back — all of the pirates. As I made my way back from the jungle to which I had escaped, my hands were tied, and I was taken to the most awful man, the leader of these vulgar and violent animals. Who laughed at me. Sitting upon a ridiculous-looking chair, something he had stolen from a family of royalty, I am sure. The pirate made it look obscene. The gold trimming around the legs and arms of the chair, a high back that the filthy pirate leaned against as he held my journal in his hands. My memoir, this book, my personal belongings spread out in front of him. I was surprised when he spoke the King's English, as I had first heard him speak the native tongue of my Spain.

"You are to be married, eh? This filthy child I see in front of me? You are too old?" He laughed with the sounds of a barkeep, the vulgar man. "I read in your book that you are old! How old could you be?" He actually grabbed a piece of my hair and twirled it around his fingers. Something so personal and so familiar. The gall of this pirate. He calls himself Jose Gaspar; he told me to call him Sir Gaspar,

what gall! He talked to me as if he had known me for a long time. I was horrified. Then, dear Lord, the bandit leaned over and whispered in my ear. I could not believe it. He told me I had too much chutzpah to live with an old man; I would be better off staying here. I slapped him. An unlikely future outcome, but I did. I slapped him. It's a blessed wonder I am here to write this. He did have the audacity to look amused and then said for them to give me my belongings. He said he had all he needed. I'm not sure what that means, but I'm going to find out. This filthy buccaneer will not get the best of me.

Winter, 1818

It may be winter; the weather does not seem to change besides rain and no rain. It may be a little cooler, and the sun is not in the sky quite as long. My Papa said the summers were forever in the New World or at least in the part to which I was traveling. I will write when I can, for no other reason than to keep my sanity. But my days are full of work and worry. I am trying to be strong for the others that are here, but I fear that it is all for naught. I am thankful that I found my Mama's Bible in my returned bag. Holding it brought back my mother's *words and gave me strength. God puts us where we are, at a time and a place for a reason. We are to follow His direction and go where He takes us. I argued with her when she told me that. I regret that now, but I still have my doubts as to her wisdom. I do know that my mother was wise, but perhaps misguided. She also thought that one day women would not be treated as property, but given the same value as a man! That day would certainly not be coming to this world; I do not believe. All of the women here are nothing more than slaves to these men.*

I have found Victoria. She is entirely addled, I fear. She walks around talking to herself and looking at something that is not there. I tried to offer comfort but found all I can do is lead her to a cot located close to mine. I can keep an eye on her. If I hand her something to do, she will do it over and over again, as stirring a pot. It is better than she sits and talks to whoever it is she sees in her broken mind.

I have been unable to find Victoria's parents or her fiancé, Master Jamison. I fear he is at the bottom of the ocean, and don't like to contemplate where her parents might be.

I have somehow become the organizer of the women in both my hut and the ones surrounding me. At least the ones coming from our ship. I realized there are other women here, from other boats, I assume. Also hostages. It is easy to discover the leader of the other women; there are two more like me that try to set up schedules and place the people where they can do what needs to be done — the preparation of the food, the cooking, the serving to the filthy pirates.

I have nodded at the other two women who try to keep their huts safe and busy, and they nod back. How I would like to have a conversation that did not involve skinning a gopher that had been thrown into the hut!

I have learned much since my time here. I have learned how to skin animals, how to prepare food that must be eaten for survival. I have learned how to lie and lie some more to these women that we will be rescued when I scarce believe it. If this is God's direction, and this is where He wants me to be, as my sweet mother would have me think, I find it hard also to believe that He cares for me.

Another day

I cannot know what day it is I write this, one day blends into another here. The sun comes up, the sun comes down, and I have no concept of how many days it has been. I will simply address it as yet another day in this wretched place.

There have been changes, small ones, but changes nonetheless. This pirate that calls himself Sir Gaspar called for my service. I had no idea of the reason and was quite afraid that he meant to accost me when I was brought to him. I was determined to show no fear, and I did not. But the brute surprised me. He asked for my counsel. Gaspar said that I stood out from the others, and he had been impressed by the words he read in my journal. Inquiring about my ability to read and write so well, it was apparent he has not been around many women who have had the opportunity to educate themselves in the proper setting.

I held myself responsive but terse. Offering little more than a short answer to his questions, he became quite agitated with me. He bade me sit down, which I refused. Told again to sit down, and pushed by one of his underlings; he rebuked the man and told him I would sit when I pleased. I looked at him curiously, and astonishing even myself, I sat.

This pirate wanted to hear of Spain, and how things were. He asked me to come each day when he was on the island at the noon meal and talk with him. I quickly asked what it was he wanted to talk about, quite sure that he would be taking liberties.

The detestable bandit that I remembered returned with a gleam in his eye as he told me that he would not touch me unless I asked to be touched. Since this, of course, was reprehensible, I relaxed and agreed on the condition that he would honor some requests that I had. I was inwardly happy that he was taken aback at my response, but he nodded and asked what those requests were.

Now I have been able to reassure the women that we will receive fresh water each day. We can go in groups to the stream nearby without interference from the raucous men and have time to rest and talk together.

The pirate assured me that he would demand that his men not force any woman into any abasement, but did say some women wanted the attention that his men were only too happy to give. When I responded that I doubted that assumption, he laughed. He told me I knew so little about the world. When I answered with a question as to why he would want to talk with me at all if he thought so little of me, he didn't answer.

Strangely, he asked that I bring the Bible with me when I returned the next day for the noon meal.

More tomorrow, maybe. I tire, and I must talk with the other two women who are leading their groups. We are working together, thankfully, to make the best of this horrendous situation in which we find ourselves.

The next day-

I am quite miserable, having concluded my day and having little daylight left to put my thoughts together and write them down. When the pirate asked me to read from my mum's Bible to him at the noon meal, I refused until he would tell me what the intentions were for all of the women on the island. And I asked what had happened to the men. The brute told me quite explicitly what was happening now, and what would happen later. Some of the men, but the pirate was not aware if Master Jamison was one of them, were sent back to Spain, in an old ship that had not been sunken or burned. The men were to tell the families of the women kept here that their loved one would be returned for the proper amount of currency. We are to be swapped, we have been kidnapped for ransom! I am sick to think of it. I must tell the others but haven't had the opportunity to talk with Antonia or Floriana, the other two women leaders here, about my talk with the pirate. I was so upset as I was reading from the Bible to him that he bade me stop and return to my hut. I could hear the anger in his voice and exited his log-hewn cabin quickly.

I must sleep. I am tired of thinking, and my body aches from the heat that has returned to the island.

Another day-

I have been trounced for my feelings about the ransom. Antonia and Floriana are singing praises and laughing with the other women. "We are going home," they told me. I suppose it is a positive way to look at it. And it quite explains why the pirates do not attack us, at least most of us. We would not be worth quite so much if we had been besmirched. All of the women are willingly going about their tasks, giddily watching the ocean for signs of a return ship.

It is almost as if they think their relatives will come toting a carpetbag filled with coin, and they will be reunited at once. I do not share their cheerfulness, although I am not sure why. Perhaps because I will not be returning to someone I love. The prospect, however, of leaving this island forever is welcoming.

The pirate Gaspar has left the island. I am not sure why or even if he shall return. Better for me, I grow tired of reading to him, and the questions the Captain of this island asks are quite personal. He shows interest in the Bible book of Acts and reacts with genuine amusement at Paul's travels and experiences. I do admit a certain amount of confusion as concerns this pirate's life. He seems quite learned and has attained a certain amount of education. He is very distant about any questions about himself. It is of no matter. I must rest. A storm is brewing, the men are saying. We must ready ourselves for a real 'blow' is what I hear in whispers.

Much later-

It has been many weeks since I have been able to write. My temperament is such that I have been unable to adequately express myself without using such vile language that I couldn't write down! I fear I am becoming quite the brazen hussy. There is no answer, but I must pray that coin reaches this shore soon so that I may be returned to my home and respectability.

We are less now. Having lost several to the mighty winds and stormwaters that blew across the island, the rest is left to clean up the mess and bury the dead, when we can find them. None can escape the smells and horrible sights, and it has been too much for some of the women. The pirates are not sympathetic and refuse food and fresh water to those that cannot bring themselves to spend their days cleaning and putting back to place the huts and living quarters. I have brought in food to those that hunger and thirst and are too weak to perform even the smallest duties, but even I have no sympathy for the criers and whiners that were gathering wood for fires and cooking only a few days ago.

The storm was beautiful as it approached from the south, a glorious sunset sending out beams across the darkening sky. The storm's power increased as it moved northward. The beauty was a lie, however. The strikes of light, even amidst the stars twinkling above, and then the winds came. The small boats were thrown upon the shore, and some were mere kindling when the winds subsided. Huts were upended and blown away. Many women and young girls held onto unstable wooden poles that did not withstand the fury of the storm. I know of only two of the men that died, pulled by the waters out to sea as they worked to save the small ship anchored just off the coast. But we have buried eleven women, and three have not yet been found. Few of the pirates lent a hand to any woman while we were being pummeled by the storm. I have thankful prayers for those that did take pity and help some to safety inland, away from the worst of the winds.

It has been three days since the storm passed on to the north, and it has cooled somewhat, thankfully. Gaspar's right hand, Slago, now considers himself king of the island, and everything and everyone on it. I suppose he believes Gaspar to be dead at sea since we have not heard from him in weeks too numerous to count, at least in this horrid place. Many of the pirates are not happy about Slago being in control, but none have mutinied. I'm not sure if it is due to their cowardice or lack of energy.

Slago is cruel, and I don't expect the women here, including myself, are going to enjoy his rule. He speaks no kindness to anyone, and barks orders to men and women alike. I have made my way as far from his presence as possible, but many have not been able to avoid his harsh tongue and pointed boot at whatever body part is most available to him.

Farris, one of the kind pirates helping the youngest to safety during the storm, has been sneaking me food and water for the women when he can. Slago has determined that the women should hunt for themselves, although I am not sure what he would have us use to kill. We are not allowed any type of weapon; even a sharpened stick is taken and broken. Without Farris, I daresay we would starve or be beaten for not having the strength to attend to Slago's desires. I, probably because of my plain looks, have not been commanded to his bed; but many of the women have been defiled since Slago has taken over. The pirates that once obeyed Gaspar's orders to keep the women pure to procure the best price remain pensive as they watch Slago defile one woman after another. After he has done with them, the other pirates circle the bewildered girl as a vulture contemplates his next meal. I have been lucky, but I do not expect to remain so.

Probably 1819

It has been another week or perhaps longer, time passes, and I know not the days. Farris has smuggled me a knife and keeps hope afloat that Gaspar will return and right the indignities brought on by Slago. I'm not sure why Farris has decided to impress upon me his confidence. Perhaps because he attended to the Pirate Gaspar's meals and abode, he feels some sympathy for this plain woman that read to his master. I admit I do miss our luncheon meals and conversations around God and what His will is for all the different peoples in the world. Gaspar had in his mind that God's will for him was hell, and of that, I was in complete agreement when we first landed on this wretched island. But I did come upon some semblance of kindness and even sadness in Gaspar's manner. He is probably dead and probably abides now in hell. It is of no matter to me. I feel unable to complete each day with a shred of dignity left, much less think about a pirate's doom.

I have so much to make note of, and my days are full. But I will try. It has been many weeks since I last wrote, and as I look back at my last entry, I am astounded at how different things are now. But I must try to fill in the spaces between, for someone may read my words and wonder at my change of direction.

As I feared, Slago eventually found his way to me. He was much bigger than Gaspar and filthy. Seldom cleaning himself or his stringy hair that hung down in his face, his smell was disgusting even to the other pirates. But they feared him, I could see it. He was loud and had a dark soul. I spent many days trying to hide those most vulnerable from him, the young and the weak girls that would not have the emotional strength to overcome the horrid indignities he would cause. He came into the hut where I was caring for a woman who had suffered from profound injuries during the storm. I shielded her from him with my body, and he looked at me at length, making me feel naked and dirty. With a gruff laugh, he grabbed my arm and pulled me to Gaspar's cabin, which Slago had taken for his own. As he readied himself by pulling at his clothes, I was able to retrieve the small knife from the band, where I kept it hidden on my leg. As he approached, I waited until I could almost feel his breath upon my face and struck out. I am not certain where I pierced his face, only that I did. He roared and stumbled backward, and I made my escape, or so I thought. He grabbed my hair and yanked me back.

I fought back, pummeling at him with my fists until he backhanded me with such force that I fell back upon the makeshift cot. I felt that my fate was sealed, but in the minute before he would have fallen onto me, Farris entered the cabin and nervously looking at me, told Slago that Gaspar was approaching.

Slago turned and stood, anger written upon his face. More than anger. Hate. "Where is he?" he growled as Farris backed up, sneaking glances at me.

"On his way from the ship, I'm told," Farris said quietly.

"You're told? TOLD? Who told you, you blabbering idiot?" Slago wrapped the filthy black cape he was fond of around his shoulders. Wiping the blood from his face where I had cut him, he sneered, "You didn't see him yourself?"

"No, no. Fyke was down there fishing, he said so," Farris looked out the door towards the water. *"It is darkening, and I don't see so well."*

"Where is Fyke? Oh, never mind. I'll gather him with the rest. We'll have a welcome for his majesty; we will." Slago strode out the door, and I could hear him barking orders as he got farther away.

Farris immediately came to my side and helped me put my cloak on over my disheveled clothing. "Hurry, 'm lady, we must go through the trees to a safer place. I fear that Gaspar will not arrive in time to set things 'aright before Slago makes his move against him." Farris hurried me through the opening in the back of the hut, and we crept through the trees until we were far enough to avoid detection.

"What is going on?" I questioned Farris. "Is Gaspar here or not? What did Slago mean? Is he going to fight Gaspar? Who is he bringing — who is 'his majesty' that Slago was talking about?"

Farris just shook his head. "Another time, lassie. You can 'git Sir Gaspar to tell you what he wants you to know. 'Fer now, let's just get us two in hiding, away from that Slago. He'll be looking for the both of us; he will."

"Why would he do that? Is Gaspar not coming?" I was confused, and Farris was not making much sense.

"He's coming; only he is still a bit further out than I opted. I saw the ship from the turret at the end of the island. That old tower is most 'down now, but I can climb up one side and see quite a bit far out." Farris continued on a broken path of shells and fronds discarded by the trees arching the narrow walkway.

I knew about the turret. I had seen it when I had tried to escape. It looked much too fragile to attempt a climb, and I had steered clear of it, fearing it was manned by one of the pirates. An old tower made of stones collected from the island itself. Not very tall, barely over 20 feet at best, it was still taller than anything else close to the water. The island itself was mostly flat from what little I could tell, with little variation.

We seemed to have walked a long way when Farris pulled me through the vines and brush to a small alcove beside a small stream. Rocks were strewn about and a waterfall, no taller than five feet, gurgled with fresh water. Farris pulled aside some limbs and vines hanging down beside the small stream falling in the pool and pointed at the opening, completely invisible before. A small opening behind the waterfall carved out from the water years ago.

"Here, this is where you go if you hear anything. You hear it, 'ye git in there!" He nodded and started to walk onward down the path. As I pulled at his sleeve, he looked back at me.

"I'm going with you! Why should I hide in there? We will both go and hide somewhere." I had no intention of staying in that tiny, closed-in space all alone.

Farris shook his head. "No, m 'lady. I will warn Gaspar of what is coming. Stay here." He reached into his belt and pulled a small pistol. Taking my hand and placing the gun in it, he asked, "Can you use this?"

"Yes." I didn't hesitate. My father, against his better judgment, had shown me the particulars of such a weapon, and I had no doubt I could and would use it if needed.

Farris nodded. "You hear anything, you 'git in there. Anything bothers you, you shoot it, yes?"

"Yes," I repeated. My voice sounded strong, but my knees were shaking, and I felt as if I couldn't take a

deep breath. As I watched Farris disappear into the jungle-like terrain, I sat down on a large stone abutting the pool of water from the stream. Lizards jumped along the rocks lining the small pond. I stared at them and remembered my avulsion to them when we first landed on this island. I now find them amusing. At such a frightening time, I found my mind going to strange thoughts. I suppose it is a reaction to fear. Looking around, I was reminded that all is not ugly and dirty on this land in the sea. The tall palm trees, the ferns waving in the breeze as a flag waves its encouragement over all that is below. The mangroves around the beaches are home to exotic wading birds and stand as soldiers of protection against the winds and destructive waves that can intrude with storms. The pirates could have saved much by not trampling the mangroves as they had done.

Listening intently, I heard nothing untoward, and my eyes sought the beauty of this place, amid the filth and pain caused by the pirates. Spain has an abundance of lush countryside with beautiful flowers, but I have seen nothing that can compare to the abundance of color and delicate petals of every hue that adorn this island. Growing wild along every path, high in the trees and flowing along the ground, the vines and tall grasses also erupt with *color and attract butterflies of beauty I have never seen. Even the lanky sea oats hold wonders, with tiny creatures living among the sand and roots of the grasses growing along the beach.*

Writing these words, I remember my fleeting feeling of peace as I sat there staring at the trickling water stream. I remember my prayer of thanksgiving. Thanking my Lord for showing me the wonder of His world in the middle of trying times. And praying that I would not die this day.

As I mentioned, the peace was short-lived. It was only a shiver up my back at first, but then I could hear voices from the trail down below. Coming my way from the pirate's domain. I moved as quietly as I could and went behind the waterfall, the cold stinging my head and eyes as I wrapped myself into a tight ball and pulled the vines and tree limbs back into place, gripping the pistol in my hands.

Two voices, one of them Slago's, thundered from the path. "He told me you told him so!" came the gruff voice of Slago.

"I told him nothing! I didn't know Gaspar's ship was out there. I was abed when you yelled for me, nowhere close to the water!" I recognized Fyke's

voice. The lie was found out. I only hoped that Farris was not found, as well.

Barely breathing at all, I heard rather than saw one of them at the water. Slurping the cold water with hands cupped, the noise was close enough I could have reached out and touched the head of the person squatting there.

Another loud slurp and then a spray of water coming into my face as a hand wiped the water from his mouth. "No matter," Slago growled, inches from my clenched fist, holding my hand around the pistol. "The tall woman, she said she saw the wench and Farris head up this way. We'll have them soon enough," Slago snarled as he rose from the water.

I held my breath as I waited for the two vile pirates to continue up the path, then crawled out from behind the brush concealing my hiding place. The cold water rushed over my face and hair again, and I shivered, though the temperature was high. I admit I was, to some extent, frantic and lost my willies about me. Pacing around the small space I felt confined to, I was uncertain whether I should follow to aid what little I could to Farris or return to the other women I had vowed to protect. I can't tell how long I waited, but the sun was sinking away, taking away my light to find the path. Finally, deciding that I must go back to the women, I started down the path and heard gunshots. The noise seemed to be coming from directly above the slight rise that Slago had taken, and then I heard the thrashing of tree limbs. I quickly returned to my hiding place behind the waterfall. Feet crunched the rocks accompanied by heavy breathing and grunts. I could hear swords flashing and an occasional shot fired.

One man overtook another on the path beside the stream, and the grunt and fall of a body into the water caused me to close my eyes tight and hold my breath. The sounds eventually fell away, and I peeked between squinting lashes to see a sword lying at my feet, having fallen through the tree limbs and vines to find my hiding place. I dared to pull the vines apart and looked on the stream where a man lay, face down in the water. I recognized the cloak. It was Farris. Choking back a sob, I tried to pull him from the water when I heard more feet coming from behind. Crawling back into my hiding place, I pulled the sword in with me. One hand with a sword, the other with the pistol, and I was unable to open my eyes. I should have recognized the voice, but did not when Farris' body was pulled from the water and "No, no, no, not you Farris." I couldn't hold back the *sob and pulled back into the hole as far as I could, knowing my cry was probably heard.*

I was right. The vines parted, and a hand closed around the pistol. I looked up and saw Gaspar, looking down at me with nothing but anguish in his eyes.

"Shush, little one. Stay here. Keep the pistol. If anyone but me comes back, shoot them." His eyes fell to the sword. He picked it up. "For Farris," he said to no one in particular and hurried down the path after the other pirates.

I have no idea of time after that. I stayed there, sometimes dozing and then awakened by the sound of yelling and gunshots. The sun was breaking through the hanging limbs, so it was morning. The misty air surrounding the high trees was ablaze with yellow light, but the air closer to the ground was wet with dew and steam rising from the fronds and leaves as the hot sun made its way down. I was cramped and needed to stretch, but was also frightened of what I would find. Gaspar was by far preferable to Slago, but I was afraid to hope for any change in the days and weeks to come. Whether by Gaspar or Slago, I was a captive. If I returned to Spain, I was a captive to a life I didn't want but had no control over.

Stretching as much as I could in my cramped space, I had decided to venture out on my own, without waiting any longer. As I parted the vines to unfold my legs, I looked up into the shaded eyes of Gaspar. Tears fell unbidden down my cheeks. The pirate reached down and pulled me up, pulling me closer to his vest and holding my head softly. I sobbed against this man whom I had nothing but contempt for. 'Not Slago,' I thought.

Gaspar continued to hold me when another of his men came onto the trail and stood waiting. "It is Farris," he said to the man. "Take him and bury him. Bury him close to the turret. He liked it." He stopped the man as he bent down to pick up Farris' body. "Treat him well." The other man nodded.

Gaspar turned to me. "You are a courageous woman, Magdalena. A very brave woman. It is safe now. I am sorry this has been a hardship for you. I expect to hear in a few days from your families. You will be going home soon. I did not," his voice caught as he sought for words, "I did not want for this to be the way it has been. I am neither good nor bad, but I do not want to be evil, you see."

"What is the difference between bad and evil? If you are one, you are the other!" I pushed away from this man who had kidnapped me and others. This

man gained profit from the crime. This man who I was sure had sent people to their death.

Gaspar looked at me with sadness in his eyes. Nodding, he pointed at the pistol. "Do you want to shoot me, m' lady?"

"No. Because I am not evil. I will not kill someone because I do not care for them, only if they are trying to kill me or hurt someone else!" I rose to my full height, which unfortunately was still several inches below his chin.

A small smile crossed Gaspar's face. "I see. So I am safe for now." He turned to go. "You may come back down and talk to the other women. They are concerned for you." He paused. "I will never hurt you, Magdalena. And Slago and those men who followed him are no more. They can do no more harm."

I am tired of writing. It has been exhausting, these past few weeks. Our lives are better, much better. The pirate Gaspar has grown an actual heart, it appears. Too little, too late. I've told him so, but he continues to stand by his word to make things better.

Master Jamison has returned. I can scarcely believe it, but it is he. He has not seen Victoria. I dread his countenance when he does. She is little more than a small child, doing what is asked if it is simple enough. She asks for 'mama' occasionally but says very little otherwise.

Master Jamison and some other men are talking with Gaspar. I was with Gaspar, reading to him when one of his men came to tell him that the ship had arrived, and the men were beginning to make arrangements. I immediately took my leave and went to inform the other women what was transpiring. The women are whispering and giggling like it was a dance they were going to, instead of a bargaining table.

I made my way to the beach. Watching the birds fly in and out of the water for their evening meal was relaxing. Life on the island has been much more pleasant. Gaspar allows the women to come and go as they please, and has the men help with essentials. Everyone is well-fed, and the only alliances are those that are agreeable to both parties. I have counseled the women to stay away from these men and prayed that God speaks to their conscience.

I have prayed for myself, as well. This Gaspar, this pirate, this man. He is much more than initially thought. He has been agreeable to answer some questions, although when I get too close, he changes the subject.

Gaspar wants redemption. He wants assurances that he will not be doomed to spend eternity in darkness but can atone for his misdeeds and earn God's forgiveness. I do not know how to counsel him. Is there redemption for such vileness? I do not know what evils he has done and am reluctant to know all things about him. Does God forgive that which man will not?

I happened upon Gaspar when he was not aware I was coming. A question had come up about the availability of a particular herb for the alligator meat, and I told the women that I would find out if we could obtain some. Not being able to find familiar herbs on the island, many of us were finding new ways to prepare meals. I have to admit that I was not just a little proud of myself on my culinary accomplishments.

Back to Gaspar. I walked in; his men made no mind of me as I entered his room. He was reading, reading aloud my mother's Bible that I had inadvertently left that morning. Reading aloud for conviction, perhaps? He read well. I considered that he didn't need me to read to him. Deep in his recitation of the Word, I silently slipped out, strange thoughts permeating my confused mind. What verses was he reading? I think it was first Timothy? I was reading from there a few days ago. He must have continued the same scripture.

I remembered the words he was reading: **'Here is a trustworthy saying that deserves full acceptance: Christ Jesus came into the world to save sinners—of whom I am the worst. But for that very reason I was shown mercy so that in me, the worst of sinners, Christ Jesus might display his immense patience as an example for those who would believe in him and receive eternal life.'**

Yes, that was it. Paul was talking to Timothy, I remember. That was it. My Lord offers mercy. My heart jumped when I thought about this. I must tell Gaspar the next time I see him. He can receive forgiveness. I was wrong to deny it. Wrong to deny that he could receive it from God. Wrong to think that I could withhold it myself. If Gaspar is truly despondent over his actions, who am I to judge?

Still, the inkling in my mind – how many has he killed? How can God put this away? My very soul is struggling. So much to think about, to pray about. And pray, I must. God answers prayers. There is proof. Master Jamison is here, is he not?

The next day

Master Jamison did indeed bring news of offers accepted and rejected. Much laughter and some tears. Gaspar sent him to me after his meeting, and it was with deep sorrow that I led him to Victoria. His tenderness towards her was enough to put all of us within earshot in tears. She had no recognition of him, nor anyone else in the room. But when he asked her to come and walk with him, she took his hand and did as he asked. I had explained to him that she had the mind of a small child, and I didn't expect that she would improve upon that condition. Master Jamison thanked me for looking after her and said something extraordinary.

"I had no hope of finding her alive at all. Feeling sure that the pirate had violated her and in all

likelihood killed her, I am thankful to the Lord that this pirate, at last, had a change of heart and is allowing me to take her home. He even expressed true sorrow, I believe, in his charge to have caused this vile thing. I am to take his fastest ship back to Spain, and hopefully back to some normalcy in her life. There is hope, Magdalena, there is always hope."

I asked him if Gaspar was going to accept the offers for the return of the women, and he couldn't give me an answer. Master Jamison simply said that Gaspar told him that he was sorry for all the trouble that he had caused and that he would ready the ship to take them back to Spain. The vessel should be ready within a week's time, with plenty of provisions for everyone.

I inquired of Victoria's parents and was told that her mother had died of a sickness on the return trip to Spain the previous year, but her father had prevailed and was home waiting for Victoria's return. The knowledge that some passengers aboard our ship had returned to Spain lightened my spirits for a few moments, at least.

I had avoided the question I was unsure about for long enough. Holding Victoria's hand and smiling at her sweet face, I asked Jamison about my situation. Had my parents made a good offer? Knowing that my intended husband would be the one approached, I also wanted to know what his offer had been. Master Jamison just shook his head. "I was under strict instructions not to divulge nor read what was in the packet," he said to me. He wouldn't look at me, so I'm not sure he was truthful.

I will find out when I meet with Gaspar, which will be soon, I have decided.

Days later

There is much to say. It was exhausting, readying the ship for transport back to Spain. The cabins available for the women were cleaned and made ready by Gaspar's men. My surprise at their attempts to prepare bedding and toiletry needs were met with apologetic grins. Most of these men were never taught the niceties. They were brought from the poorest of society to follow pirates and vagabonds around the globe as a way of life. Gaspar was appealing to their better nature, I supposed. The ship left with much ado. I was amused at some of the women actually hugging men, with a respectable distance between them, of course, the same pirates they had feared a few months before.

There is a new man on the island, a missionary from England. He arrived on a small ship a few days after Master Jamison. He is holding services, and with each time he opens the doors to the small building he has made his chapel, more of the pirates venture in. It is continuing to be a strange group here. Gaspar brought the man; I assumed to help him find his absolution from his sins. Father Jacob is found in Gaspar's company daily. I haven't had the opportunity to talk with the priest privately, but intend to do so, for my own personal reasons.

The ship has gone. Most of the women have left, except for a few that entertained the idea of staying or were agreeable to taking the next boat, as cabins were full. I have not decided what my fate shall be.

As I read through this journal, I realize that there is much that is left out. Many of the little things that should be noted, which can become big things.

I have changed on this island. I no longer fret about my hair; it is fine as long as it is clean and pulled back, affording me the sun on my face. It is still black but seems to have developed some red strands, which I'm sure is attributed to the sunshine that beats down upon us most days. I don't mind the sunlight; I have adjusted myself to the heat and enjoy the feel of the cool ocean water during a particularly humid day. My skin is darker than before, although I stay covered during the brightest part of the day to prevent the burn that kept me in pain in the beginning. The pirates seem to have burned and burned again until their skin is leather-like.

My hands, once so delicate and dainty, are now calloused and scarred from daily activities and preparing meals. My body is stronger, even with the change in diet I have experienced since leaving Spain. The water jugs that I could hardly lift when I first landed on this island are now light and swing easily from my arms.

The change is not only on the outside. I suspect I have grown as a woman does, but I have also faced some unpleasant traits about myself. Much of my wasted time in Spain was spent in front of a mirror. I disliked the way I looked and yearned to be beautiful. I accepted my fate of marrying an old man to appease my father and did not consider any other course. I wanted to trust my mother when she said that one day women would be appreciated and treated differently, but privately I believed the words unspoken by the men in my life. Women were basically the property of men and should defer at all times to their requests, understanding that it was more of a mandate than a plea.

I have spent hours thinking about these things, looking at the world around me. This island, which was once a prison, has proclaimed its beauty in big and little ways. From the smallest flowers to the largest of the majestic palms, stunning revelations of the island's quiet majesty surrounds me. The butterflies, from flower to flower, the strange birds that inhabit the lakes and wade in the ocean; all remind me of something bigger. Of God. I see beauty here and have no need to look into a mirror in search of beauty in myself. God created me, so I am beautiful. Just as each butterfly that drapes the magnificent wings across the petals of the hibiscus is beautiful. I belong to God, so I am no one's property. None but His.

I have read, although mostly at the request of the pirate, my mother's Bible more thoroughly than ever before. I have found the Word printed there to have a significant impact on me.

Will the words in this journal ever be read by another? I have returned to the beginning and seen that while I have neglected to place the most *importance on things that should be uppermost on my mind, I also find myself thinking selfishly of what I want for myself. I have not yet decided what my course of action will be. I don't want to return to Spain until I have chosen my fate. Gaspar offered me the finest cabin on the ship ready to sail, but I declined. Saying I would wait until the next one and give up a cabin for another might have seemed to be unselfish, but in truth, I did not want to leave just yet.*

I had approached Gaspar about the packet sent from Spain and about the price agreed upon for me.

My Padre had deferred to Francisco de Villagron, my betrothed in Spain. Although I had only seen this man once across a hallway, my father must have considered me no longer under his charge and determined to let a man I had not even met determine my fate.

Gaspar held the letter from my father in front of him as he read it aloud and offered it to me. Unable to speak, I shook my head, and Gaspar laid the letter down. Hurt and despair pulled at the breath in my lungs. What had my mama' said? Or did she have any say in the matter? I took a deep breath and asked Gaspar if there was a letter from de Villagron. He held it out to me. I should have included my fiancé's message in this journal, but I couldn't bear to keep it.

My betrothed stated that he would consider payment if certain conditions existed. Notably that I had not been defiled and would be expected to prove that with a doctor's visit upon my return to Spain. Also, he insisted that I should not have been diminished to the point that I would be unable to care for his four children from his previous marriages. I did not know there were any children involved and was not aware that he had been married before. His last two wives had died and had produced four children. It was clear what my purpose was to be.

As I finished reading and lowered the letter to my lap, my eyes stinging with tears, Gaspar inquired as to what I should like to do. Not realizing that he was asking and not telling me, I could do nothing but shake my head. As luck would have it, Gaspar had a rare fire burning in the rock fireplace in the corner. I walked over and placed the letter in the flames. Whatever I was to do, it would not be marrying de Villagron. My father would be furious.

Thankful that Gaspar has not pressed me for my plans, I am considering what few options I have. When I return to Spain, my father will have no choice but to accept me back into his home. At least, I think that he will take me back, even though it will be begrudgingly. My prospects do not look promising. What will I do when I return? Father will most assuredly be upset. The likelihood that he will try to marry me off to another is paramount in my mind. I could teach. My education is such that I would likely be able to contract as a teacher.

Is that what I want my life to be? I don't know. I have never given much thought to what I would like to do, always assuming the future was determined for me by others. This will require much thinking and much prayer.

The next day

As I read over what I had written yesterday, I can see the indecision in my words. Still undecided, there are other options I was not aware of.

Gaspar sent word early that he would like to speak with me after the morning meal. I made no rush about it, but the pirate sitting at Gaspar's door opened it for me when I arrived shortly after that. As I walked in, Gaspar was cutting a mango with a large knife. Offering part of the fruit to me, he motioned towards the chair across the table. To his credit, he took his feet off the corner of the table when I walked in.

"I talked to the Father about you," Gaspar started talking before I had sat down. He sputtered, seeming as if he needed to get it out before he forgot what to say.

"Father Jacob can use you, and he said he would look out for you, and you can help him with his duties as a, uh, a priest."

I was amused at first, and then thought I understood where the conversation was headed. "Do you think I should be a nun?" I asked Gaspar.

"Blimey! No, woman! You, a sister? I think not," Gaspar was exasperated.

I was quite taken aback at his expression. He finally gathered himself together and said that I could stay on the island and work with Father Jacob if I did not want to return to Spain.

I inquired about the payment. I obviously did not have funds to pay him for my ransom.

Gaspar stood up suddenly and said that it was not of any importance. It was so bizarre. I left his room *with the direction to let him know of my decision before the next ship sailed in two days' time.*

I have a lot of thinking to do.

August 14, 1819

As you see, I know the date! Father Jacob brought with him a printed calendar, one which I have never seen. Of course, our Spanish style differs from that of Pope Pius. I was able to copy it so that I would honestly know the date. A very simple thing, really, but I noticed it each time I wrote recollections for this log.

I remain on the island. The ship Neptuno left for Spain this morning after all the remaining women and girls that wanted to return to their homeland had boarded. I am residing with three other young women, all of whom did not receive a packet from home with an answer to the ransom. They also are determined to stay here in the Americas. Gaspar has assured all of us that he will have us taken to St. Augustine should we so desire. Otherwise, we are free to remain here, tend to our small cottage such as it is, help Father Jacob, and do other duties such as cooking and mending. We are, surprisingly enough, treated respectfully by his men. Several other women, many of whom have been here longer than I reside in another building on the other side of the small settlement here. I understand that the men frequent their home and have meals and commence other activities I would rather not entertain. Father Jacob says that the frequency has substantially lessened, however. I have no doubt that it is his hope, but I am not sure it is true.

I have determined that I will stay here in these Americas. There is much talk about the wildness and beauty of this land. I wish to explore. There are, of course, also cities with exquisite homes and bountiful harvests. I have no wish to move to a town. I have had quite enough of the intricacies of city people. These pirates are wild and ruthless, yes, and some of them are quite violent. But some are no more than children themselves, and with the proper person in charge, they may yet have a positive impact on lives around them. Father Jacob has great hope.

Gaspar himself is a mystery. He has asked that I continue my reading, and seems to enjoy our discussions about the possibilities of heaven and hell. Atonement is not a subject he yields to easily but has indicated by his actions that it is what he desires.

I am working with my roommates, Belle, Elena, and Sofia, to prepare a meal tonight to share. With the abundance of fresh vegetables and fruits brought by the Neptuno, put together with the fish caught today, we will indeed have a feast. Belle and Elena are sisters and were oddly happy to stay here. Sofia cried and could not be consoled for days, but is on the mend now. She is young and could not understand why her guardian would not send for her. It is odd that she is not entirely sure of her age but believes that she is of thirteen years. Belle has taken her under her wing and is presently teaching Sofia to separate the fish meat from the bones. I must attend to my duties. I did want to attest that I will lay my head down this night with content.

August 21, 1819

After taking the evening meal, I had retreated to the small chapel to read and find some quiet after the busy day. A large alligator was brought in by several of the men, and Elena and I were interested in the preparation of this massive animal for cooking. Alligator meat is quite tasty, and I was pleasantly surprised at the skills of the pirates to season and prepare the meat. We were also instructed on the procedures to salt and preserve the meat for future meals.

As I opened my Bible to read, I heard the soft voice of Father Jacob. Thinking I was alone, I did not see him sitting in the far corner talking with another. As Father Jacob and his visitor stood, I was surprised to see Belle stand with him. His words barely reached my ears. 'Of course, I will be your chaperone, my dear. Why don't we say tomorrow evening around dusk?' Belle nodded and hurried out, not noticing my presence. Father Jacob saw me as he walked over to light candles to keep out the approaching darkness.

"Father, hello. I did not mean to interrupt your conversation. I was not aware anyone was here until I had already sat down," I told him immediately. I certainly did not want him to think I was intruding on personal matters.

He smiled his kind smile and sat down beside me, saying that he was quite sure Belle would be telling me what she had spoken to him about, so he would leave it to her.

Our conversation was short but interesting. Father Jacob's inquiry about my readings with Gaspar was surprising. I assumed that Gaspar talked to him about his questions of the Bible also. But he said no, although counsel had been offered. Father said Gaspar told him he enjoyed hearing the interpretations of someone not so close to God, as he felt Father was. I was speechless at this, but Father just laughed.

'This pirate,' he said to me, 'is very special, don't you think? God has put a mark on him. One he cannot deny, though he tries, I don't doubt. Pray, Magdalena, pray for his soul.'

I had no idea how to respond to that but garnered up enough of myself that I was able to tell the Father that I did pray every day for all of us in the settlement. I told him how happy I was that Gaspar had not brought any other women to be ransomed off, and felt that was a good sign.

Father Jacob put his hand on my arm and patted it gently. 'My dear,' he said, 'you should know that Gaspar has had a change of heart about how he conducts his business. Oh yes, he remains a pirate, I suppose we will have to work hard to change that, but there are pirates, and then there are pirates.'

With that strange statement, Father Jacob stood and took his leave of me. Bewildered, I sat there a long time contemplating his words. Finally, looking for answers myself, I opened Mama's Bible. The words jumped off the page from 1 Timothy: *'I **exhort, therefore, that, first of all, supplications, prayers, intercessions, and giving of thanks, be made for all men'**. That's it.* I was to pray. God had proven himself over and over again to me, had He not? I prayed for deliverance from the storm. I prayed for Master Jamison to return for Victoria. I prayed for deliverance from Slago, from the pirates, from this island. But God knew what was best for me! How can I not pray when His Word tells me to do so. And pray for what He wishes?

I look for answers, and when I open my Mama's Bible, I almost always find them. And if I don't see a solution, I know that God hears and will answer in His time.

August 29, 1819

I am learning much about my surroundings, and about the others on this island. I am reminded that there have been changes in my living arrangements, and I have been remiss in not writing it down. Belle and her adopted daughter, Sofia, are no longer in our cabin. Belle was courted by a young man named Antonio under the courteous *supervision of Father Jacob for all of two weeks before she was wed to him. It was quite the trial to pull the information out of her, and she seemed very embarrassed when I guessed that her secret with Father Jacob was about a man. Belle said that she didn't want to offend me and talk about her attraction to a man. She assured me he had shown her respect and courtesy. She called me 'a genteel lady' that would not want to hear such things. I laughed quite heartily at that – me, a genteel lady! – and then rebuked her with a smile. After all, did we not enjoy watching men butcher an alligator and have an interest in seeing the innards strewn about? A genteel lady, indeed! We had a good laugh about it.*

I admit that I joked with her mercilessly up until her marriage vows were taken, there in the quaint chapel with the sacred words given by Father Jacob. I think I may have embarrassed her somewhat.

Many of the pirates attended, as well as women from the cottage on the other side of the settlement. Gaspar was there and uncharacteristically escorted both Elena and me to the front of the chapel for the ceremony.

There was a great feast afterward. This was a first for our small community of pirates, a priest, and women from other parts of the world. Two of the women from a separate cottage, arm in arm with uncomfortable-looking pirates, approached Father Jacob about their own nuptials, which he heartily agreed to perform soon. As we finished our feast, and the men began singing silly songs, Elena and I began to pick up the scraps to give to the large cat-like creatures that crept around the buildings late at night. It had been my misfortune to see one moving kittens – quite large ones, to be sure – and I had been feeding them ever since. Being admonished that to do so was not only ludicrous but also dangerous, I have not been deterred. Elena agrees to help me pick up scraps, but not to set the leftover food out herself.

I told Elena that I was heading back to our cottage and would drop off the pail of scraps at the tree line. Knowing she wanted to stay and listen to the songs the pirates were using to encourage the women to dance, I just smiled and told her to be careful when she made her way back to our home.

The short walk to the tree line gave me time to stare up at the starlit sky, bright with a full moon. Sunset had not been long before; the sky would be ablaze with stars within another hour. Gaspar startled me with his 'ahem,' clearing his throat to announce his presence behind me.

When I turned and looked at him, he was staring at me with a frown upon his face. I noticed that he had cut his black hair, the white streaks more prominent when short. His beard had been trimmed to a more appropriate and attractive length. His eyes were dark and unsettling, his hand resting upon his sword hilt. As I started to speak, he held up his other hand to his mouth, motioning for me to remain silent. I watched with disquiet as he walked slowly toward me, raising the sword high over my head. Why I did not scream, I cannot imagine. But thankfully, I did not. One quick motion of his sword and a snake lay dead at my feet. A moment before, it had been swinging from a branch above my head.

My breath was caught; my hand went up. Clawing at my throat, I was further alarmed when Gaspar pulled me toward him and held me tight against his chest. My throat opened, and I found I could breathe again. I stayed where I was. I admit I did not want to leave the security his embrace afforded me. My hands found the lapels of his jacket, and I grasped them, keeping him close to me, my head buried in the tight muscle between his shoulder and chest.

Gaspar was making soothing sounds. I can't recall if there were any actual words spoken. I sensed more than felt him begin to break the embrace, and I pulled him back, not wanting to lift my head and lose the moment. I felt his hand on my head as he gently pulled my face back to look up into his eyes. The smolder there was hypnotic. My breath caught as he looked at me, his head bending ever so slowly to me. Suddenly, without warning, he thrust me back, away from him. I let out a strange sound, almost a moan as he turned around quickly, his back to me. Not knowing the ways of men, I was most embarrassed. I suppose that I was inappropriate or only too unappealing for him to see me as anything but a girl that no one wanted. He didn't immediately walk away, however.

Gaspar never turned back to me, only said over his shoulder that he would like to see me the next day after the morning meal, and to bring my Bible.

I do not know what to pray for. Back here in my makeshift bed, glad that Elena has not yet made it back, I alone can contemplate my behavior tonight. Gaspar is a pirate! Perhaps a reformed one, maybe not. And I was throwing myself in his arms!

The day will always be a blur upon my soul. It will do no one kindness to report on the happenings of the day, or the days before, but I feel I must at least give recognition of those lost.

I hurried through my morning meal, having decided to distract Gaspar by apologizing for my behavior and begging his pardon to forget my forwardness of the night before. Good intentions were discarded as soon as I walked into the room where Gaspar sat staring out the open wall to the seagrass and beach a short walk away.

He turned and looked at me with a thoughtful expression upon his face. At least he didn't appear to be angry or disgusted, so I walked over, sitting down and placing the Bible on the table in front of me.

"Let us read more about King David today," he told me, a small smile upon his face. Gaspar is very interested in King David, in all of his exploits and the various ways he seems to defy God. He has asked me multiple times if God has forgiven David for his transgressions. However, this day we were

interrupted before we could begin our reading of scripture.

"Captain, sir, we got to talk," the gruff man said when he burst into the room. I recognized him as the one they called Monk. Gaspar had taken him to replace Farris as his second. I did not know him as I had Farris, but Father Jacob said that Gaspar trusted him. Elena had been making eyes at him, giggling when I teased her.

"It's not something that can wait until I am through with my morning, uh, morning visit?" I looked at Gaspar when he said that. Is that what he calls our Bible reading time? A morning visit?

"Nah, non, Captain. It's uh, really, no. Now, if you please, Captain," Monk said and acted almost afraid of Gaspar. I was surprised. Farris had never shown fear, only respect for Gaspar.

Gaspar nodded to me, and I rose to leave. I told him I would come back later if he wished. He just nodded and turned to Monk. I made my way out of the room and was walking the pathway to my cottage when I heard Gaspar's roar. Never have I heard his anger as this. It was quite frightening. I changed my direction and ran over to the chapel, hoping to find Father Jacob. Father, having heard *the thunder of Gaspar's voice, was coming out as I approached. Nodding at me, he turned and hurried to Gaspar.*

I sat there in the chapel for hours. The morning fell away to the afternoon, and the sun was sitting low in the sky when Father Jacob returned. I had heard voices yelling and preparations for something going on outside in our little village. I did not want to leave the chapel. Somehow I knew that this would be an evil thing.

Father Jacob was haggard as he walked back into the small chapel, his head hanging down. He seemed surprised to see me there and smiled a sad smile as he sat down beside me. Taking my hands in his, he let out a long sigh.

'The first ship that left, the Lady Mariana, carrying most of the women back to Spain and England; it is lost,' he said. The Neptuno caught up to another ship that passed the word along. The men, the pirates that Gaspar ordered to take the women back, mutinied against his charge and refused to turn the women over without payment, raising the ransoms due from the previous contracts. They fired upon the frigate sent to make the exchange, and the frigate returned fire. All onboard the pirate ship were lost.

My breath caught, and with tears streaming down my face, I bowed my head as Father told me how livid Gaspar had been. I couldn't bear to hear him saying how he had prayed with Gaspar and tried to help him calm his anger.

"Why do you care how he calms his anger? He is angry because he lost money! He is a dirty rotten pirate. It is his fault those people are dead! Master Jamison and Victoria! And all the others! No, do not tell me how you are trying to calm him!" I was outraged and could not contain my complete astonishment at Father Jacob's words. I should not have yelled at the Father, but I meant the words, every word.

Father Jacob just sat there, shaking his head as I ranted. I stood and ran towards the door and saw Gaspar standing there, obviously listening to me. I ran past him, pushing him aside.

I made a mistake, staying here. I should have left on the Neptuno.

September 3, 1819

Gaspar has left the island. He took a small canoe and left by himself. Those pirates that are left are unsure what to do, and have turned to Father Jacob for guidance, which is a good thing, I suppose.

A small group of pirates left upon learning of the mutiny will not return for many weeks. They are to search for any survivors and return them to Gaspar. Father Jacob said that they were to also escort the Neptuno safely to England, where she would debark her passengers.

Father Jacob approached me yesterday, giving me time to vent my anger, and asked to speak with me.

I was hesitant, but couldn't possibly refuse the request of a priest, so I listened. I am not sure how I feel about what he has told me, and also not sure that I believe it all. Not that Father Jacob would lie to me, but I do wonder if the pirate has perhaps misled him.

I am not quite as confident as Father Jacob that Gaspar has been reborn into our Lord Jesus. Gaspar told him that he had returned the contracts on the women returned, not expecting any payment, and would no longer use women as a means to fund his exploits on the water and the island. 'Gaspar saw his sin and was bereft by it,' Father Jacob said. I asked Father Jacob how Gaspar and his unruly pirates would finance their life here on the island and at sea, and Father Jacob just shrugged, which I assume means he will still raid seagoing vessels for their wares and jewels. 'Gaspar told me he would not allow lives forfeited in his name,' Father Jacob said, imploring me to forgive him for the lives he had already taken!

I am sure that Father Jacob could see that I was not taken in by the ludicrous promises made by a pirate to a priest, but just the same, he bade me ask Gaspar about his story. How he came to be on this island, the island others are calling 'Captiva.' Monk told me this. He had heard the name 'Captiva' because of the captives kept here by Gaspar. I'm sure the righteous pirate will be pleased.

I have no interest in hearing Gaspar's story. What comfort is there in knowing how a pirate came to be a pirate? It will not bring back Victoria or Master Jamison.

I want my mama'. I have missed her many times since I left Spain, but none as much as now.

September 18, 1819

Gaspar has returned. Thankfully, he is keeping to himself and has not made any demands upon me *or anyone else to my knowledge. I know that Father Jacob has approached him several times, but has not yet been able to talk with him in private.*

I cannot convince any other to join me, but I have decided that I will make my way to St. Augustine. I understand that it is charming and inviting to young women who desire to make a life for themselves. Monk told me this but asserted that it was not for me. I said that I would make my own choices, and appropriately rebuked, he didn't contradict me.

I have been helping Father Jacob ready the chapel and kitchens for any coming storms, building a supply of cured meats and vegetables that will hopefully provide food. Father has built additional benches and cots for those that may need them.

Everyone is excited about the new baby expected soon. Belle and her husband are walking around slowly, proudly showing off the large bump Belle carries in front. Completely inappropriate in Spain and England, it seems quite fitting for our island community to rejoice at the new life and display it for all. I have made plans to stay until the baby is born when I hope to convince Belle to let me take Sophia with me to St. Augustine, if only for a visit.

There are only 40 or 50 of us in our settlement, including the women and pirates, Father Jacob, and the few miscreants that have managed to stow away on a ship. It does not seem that all of the pirates are here all of the time, they appear to take turns on their vessels, ravaging and pillaging others. Thankfully once they are on the island, they do not exhibit those traits I find so objectionable. While certainly not genteel mannered and well-read, they are polite and helpful when asked. Father Jacob has done much to instill upon these wild men the gentler ways of treating women. I am thankful for Father Jacob and his wisdom and keen ability to communicate with these pirates. I can converse with most of them, but all seem reluctant to engage in much conversation with me, probably because I detest their captain.

October 10, 1819

I am back in my little cottage. Elena has finally fallen asleep, after sobbing into her coverlet for so very long. Burning a candle to write by, I cannot find sleep, though my body aches with the tiredness of extended wakefulness and stress. Our little community here has been raided by another pirate, one they called Lafitte. It looked as if we were going to be bound to this Lafitte pirate for our very lives until Gaspar charged after him with his sword. The two pirates seem to gleefully approach each other and commence the most bloody and cruel contest I have witnessed. The other men, pirates led by both Gaspar and Lafitte, cheered and yelled as if this was an event for pleasure. All of the women were horrified, to the extent that Antonio removed his very pregnant Belle to the rear of the activity, under the watchful eye of one of Lafitte's pirates, sword drawn. Lafitte would charge at Gaspar, threatening to tie him up and have him watch as they pillaged, raped, and killed all the rest of us. Gaspar would lunge back, promising death to all dear to Lafitte should any misfortune fall to anyone there. Lafitte's laughter was frightening, how I would imagine a demon to sound. Both pirates had been cut, but none too deeply to stop the progression of the duel.

Even though the fight was almost too brutal to watch, I listened intently. Gaspar threatened Lafitte's brother, Pierre, with certain death should any harm come to his men, and then jokingly asked if France would allow him to return since he had so sullied his family's name. Lafitte, in return, asked Gaspar if he still stood for the Royal Navy of Spain and if sweet Rosalia was waiting for him back home. Gaspar lunged for Lafitte's heart when Lafitte asked after King Charles, but Lafitte dodged the blade and stepped to the side. At that moment, both swords found their mark against the other's neck. Lafitte was the first to speak.

"Jose?" was all he said. "Jean?" Gaspar replied. Both men lowered their swords and bowed. I couldn't imagine what this strange turn of events would mean. Gaspar turned to Monk and said something, then motioned to Lafitte, and the two men went into his cabin.

Monk watched as they entered and closed the door. Turning back to the rest of us, "Everything stops until they come back. You can drink what we have but leave the women alone. No fighting!"

One of Lafitte's pirates leaned over to Elena and grabbed her buttocks. "I'll have ye later, lass!" he said, then backed up when Monk came toward him, laughing and yelling for something to drink.

Elena grabbed my hand and didn't stop shaking until I took her by the hand and sat her down on a bench far away from the rest. As Monk approached, I shook my head, but he continued until he was in front of Elena. Bending down in front of her, he took her hand. "M' lady, no harm shall come to you, or it will be me' dead body they come over." Elena smiled through her tears. I had not realized that she had feelings for this man, this overgrown child!

Father Jacob came up behind us, startling me when he laid his hand on my shoulder. "They are talking, and it sounds as if they are laughing and telling stories. I think it will be all right. We must be vigilant of the others, however." I told Father Jacob that I had looked for him, but he said that he had hung back with Monk, waiting for Gaspar to lead the way.

We were afraid to leave and go to our cabins, as we couldn't be sure we wouldn't be followed. So we sat and waited. The pirate that had accosted Elena returned and challenged Monk to a duel over his right to bed her, and it appeared that the fight would happen in front of us, despite Father Jacob's desperate attempts to calm the situation. As the two stood with the swords drawn and others gathered around, the pirates cheering and the women crying, I realized that this would not end well. Running to Gaspar's cabin, I opened the door, and uninvited walked in. Quickly assessing that the two pirates were drinking and not openly hostile towards each other, I was loud and frank. Telling Gaspar that his second, Monk, was likely to end up on the wrong end of the sword defending his woman *if he did not quit his childish games and come outside, I turned around and walked out. I could hear Lafitte laughing as I ran back to the continuing duel.*

Elena was on her knees on the ground, begging them to stop. I gathered her up as Gaspar strode into the fray and yelled something quite strange. He called them both 'chowder-heads' and told them the grog would end for them if they took one more swing. Both men lowered their swords, and thankfully, the fray had ended. Neither of them had a scratch, but both were vocal in their interpretation of what had transpired. Gaspar reached out to Elena and asked her if all was well. She nodded, and he looked at me. He very politely asked me to take her back to our cabin and tend to her.

Which comes to now. I haven't heard any voices in the last few minutes, so I am hoping that Lafitte's pirates are gone. They must have come from the other side of the island; I haven't seen a ship in the distance from our side. All is quiet outside. I am finally finding it difficult to hold my eyes open.

October 11, 1819

I finally laid my head down last night, but my last thought was of all the blood I saw on both Gaspar and Lafitte when I interrupted them in Gaspar's cabin.

After I had risen and made sure that Elena was still sleeping soundly, I made my way to the chapel. I felt confident that Father Jacob would know what had transpired after I had taken Elena to her bed. I was right in my assumption.

Father Jacob was on his way out the door when I arrived, carrying swathes in his arms, as well as a jug of water from his room. When I asked where he was headed, he motioned me to follow him and handed me the bandages. We were headed to Gaspar's room, he told me, where we would need to change his dressings and try to clean the wounds. Gaspar had also been vomiting, black vomit was what Father Jacob called it, and I can only assume that this is not a proper elimination of bad food. I followed, not because I particularly wanted to help, but because I could not deny Father Jacob.

Gaspar was not conscious, at least not in the present. He was rambling in his speech and burning with fever. I told Father Jacob that I did not realize that Gaspar was hurt quite so badly the night before. "Nor me, child," he said. Gaspar was not completely naked, his breeches were still attached, although they had been cut off one leg. His chest was soaked with blood. I helped Father Jacob as he instructed, removing bandages and cleaning the wounds. There were many of them. We used some of the grog left in Gaspar's cabin the night before to pour onto the wounds, at which time Gaspar moaned and seemed to go to sleep. After we had completed our work and the wounds were no longer leaking from under their bandage, we sat on the bench just outside Gaspar's cabin.

Father Jacob asked if I could sit with Gaspar while he rested for a short while. He had been attending Gaspar throughout the night. I told him that I would do so if I could go and tell Elena where I would be. I was still quite concerned about her.

After I returned, Father Jacob wearily rose from the bench and headed to the chapel as his sleeping quarter was in the rear of the chapel. I agreed to check in with Gaspar quite often to make sure he was resting comfortably and did not need his dressings changed.

I went into the cabin and pulled a chair next to his bed. Watching the trembling rise and fall of his chest, it was apparent he was in distress, but I had no idea how to administer aid. I fretted for a few minutes and then got down on my knees. Prayer.

That is what we all come to when we have no answers. My Mama' told me that when I was very young.

As I raised my eyes to Gaspar, I remembered something from my childhood. I had been very ill from a sickness that caused my chest to ache and my breathing to be very shallow. Finding that I could breathe better from a raised position, I could sleep with blankets and pillows piled behind my back.

It was challenging to maneuver Gaspar. He is a large man, and while not fat, he was heavy to move. I finally managed to raise him enough that he seemed to be breathing easier and settled into a less troubled sleep.

I took several turns around the village and returned each time to Gaspar's bedside, surely to do nothing more than Father Jacob's bidding. But I found my eyes pulled to his sleeping face. He didn't look so terrible when asleep. He was quite handsome, although he certainly would much more appealing without the blood splatter on his face.

My eyes must have grown tired because I next remember Father Jacob shaking my shoulder. As I rose my head from the bedside, Gaspar's hand fell to the side. His hand had been on my head, and I hadn't known he had awakened. He was sleeping. I nodded to Father Jacob and left to return to my duties. I had to prepare meals and knew that I could contemplate these things tonight as I write it down. Am I growing soft? I must pray for a very long time this night.

October 25, 1819

I read back over the pages here and realize that should anyone read this, they would think me quite the flibbertigibbet. My mind jumps around, and my feelings are quite uncertain. Should I throw this thing out? Not now. One day when I am old and have grandchildren, I will decide to throw it out before I die so that no one will ever see my frivolity. But for now, it gives me my past for recollection whenever I choose.

Gaspar is on the mend, and much has transpired. We have become comfortable around one another, as I spent many days attending to his needs until he was able to fend for himself. Father Jacob has been his counselor and acting 'captain' in his absence, although Monk considers himself to be doing the same. Both of them aspire to mend Gaspar in their *way, both physically and spiritually. It is quite the game to watch them fawn over him.*

As to Lafitte, Gaspar said there was a gentleman's agreement between the two men, which had been in place for several years, to avoid the other's charges. Actions of the ship Lady Marina, which brought out the English frigate, had broken that agreement. Lafitte was not aware that the pirates Gaspar had sent on the ship had mutinied against Gaspar himself.

There was much to learn, and as I had a captive audience in Gaspar, I would ask questions and refuse to do whatever chore he needed until he answered. Between the answers I received from Gaspar, and the refreshing of the tales from Father Jacob, I have pieced together a little history.

It is worth it to note here that Captain Jose Gasparilla was a captain of the Royal Navy of Spain, serving under King Charles IV. A very young man to reach the command of Captain, he was also very rash in his dealings with women of the court. His prestigious family were guests of King Charles IV on occasion, and he considered himself too valuable for his interest in one particular lady to bode him any ill. That Captain, young Gaspar, fell in love with Rosalia, who was betrothed to a court officer. With all good intentions, he spoke for her hand and asked her to disavow her previous betrothal. He was unaware that Rosalia had no intention of damaging her pending marriage to a high-ranking court officer, and was only toying with Gaspar's attentions. To avoid any scandal to herself, Rosalia levied false charges against Gaspar, involving theft of the crown jewels. Facing arrest from a farce concocted by his beloved, he stole a ship from the royal fleet and left Spain. His revenge was the capture of women on ships that had left Spain and receiving bounty for their return. The booty collected amassed a considerable fortune that Gaspar did not need for himself but supplied his pirates and ships with all needs and wants.

My total inability to refrain from rebuking Gaspar for being such a dupe was not met with appreciation for my deductive powers. I find myself looking at him as a child sometimes. Not often enough, I fear.

We are reading; we are reading every day. In the beginning, when he was unable to stand for any extension of time, he would read to me as I went about cooking and cleaning. As he was able to come outside for short periods, we would sit on the bench outside his cabin, and I would read to him.

We read the Bible most often, followed by conversations and usually disagreements on the meaning of the scripture. Gaspar had not shared with anyone his collection of books, stored away in a trunk, surprisingly in good shape. I am rereading Gulliver's Travels now; both of us had enjoyed it before. I am anxious to read a new book that I heard about from new arrivals to the island. Jane Austen wrote this wonderful book, I'm told, called Pride and Prejudice. Gaspar assured me it would arrive on the next ship.

I am sure I am rambling and sound like a young girl pining after a prince. At any rate, my feelings will remain close to my heart for the time being, whatever they are. Gaspar is planning another trip; he is mending quickly and hopes to leave within the next few weeks. He is not amicably sharing his destination or purpose, so I sit here ready to close my eyes, feeling rejected. It is not a good feeling.

November 1, 1819

I arrived at the chapel this morning, not realizing the date. Father Jacob had lit candles, and there were several sitting on benches. I walked up to Father Jacob as he finished praying with one man and tapped him on the shoulder. I asked what was going on, and he looked at me as if I had temporarily gone blind. After he informed me it was All Saints' Day, I was horrified. I had missed last year, not knowing the date, and here I was, ignoring this most Holy Day. There were so many dead to remember. I lit candles for Victoria and Master Jamison and every other person I could name that had been on the first ship to sail back to Spain. I prayed that the next boat reached England safely, and her passengers were safely on land and with their family.

As I rose from my knees, I looked around at the others in the small chapel. Mostly men, with a few of the women with them, kneeling and praying. These were pirates. Pirates that believed in God? It seemed almost insane. But I remembered my grandmother's wisdom. She had told me that many believed but did not walk with Him daily. Their belief was the strongest when the eyes of the world were closed to them, and their time was near. I had asked her if those people would find God's favor and receive eternity. She had looked at me with old, cloudy eyes and said quite plainly that no one knows what is in a person's heart but God. He alone is the judge.

I found Father Jacob again and asked about Gaspar if he had been into the chapel. He said that Gaspar preferred to grieve alone and had left for the turret to place a candle on Farris' grave. I was glad that he had not yet left for his journey but knew that he would leave soon, probably without a goodbye.

November 9, 1819

I am back in my bed this night. What wonders I have to tell! I may not be able to destroy this book even yet in my old age. As I read back to my first entry, such a young girl and so naïve, and it was only a little over a year ago! I have become a woman with a woman's heart for a man. In this short time, and a man of whom I am not sure God would approve.

Gaspar did take a trip, a very short one, with me alone. We set about in a small canoe yester morn, and Gaspar rowed us around the other side of the island. A small waterway separated Captiva from another island. I could almost see the bottom of the water as we made our way around the tip to a shoreline on the new island. Gaspar pulled up the canoe and held out his hand to help me get out and walk on the sand.

'Sanibel' he called it. We walked along the sandy shore, blemished with shells of every shape and size. I found I liked the shells better than the pristine beaches found in Spain. The mangroves and beautiful flowers jeweled in the bushes native on the island are incredible. The island was off-limits to the pirates, he told me. The only ones on the island were a few natives, leftover from a tribe of Calusa Indians that had all but been eradicated by disease many years before. There had been others there, Gaspar told me, but presently it was only the few Calusa and him. He said he needed the island to remain as it was. But he could not explain the reason. I think it is something felt and not spoken. Like faith, perhaps.

He had built a small cabin on the far end of the island. A cottage to which we retreated after watching an incredible sunset. Gaspar assured me that the sunrise would be even more spectacular, coming up over the water. Pointing to the farthest point, he said there was land there, Florida.

I was hesitant as we entered the cabin, not knowing what to expect from this man. Gaspar immediately, thankfully, put my mind at ease. Saying we would be staying the night, but that I would be inside while he was outside brought many feelings into my heart

— one of thankfulness in prayer, and one of just a little disappointment. I had yet to feel his kiss upon my lips and found myself fantasizing about it.

The small cabin had a fireplace, although I doubted that there were many instances of needing the heat. Gaspar built a fire, however, and had brought strips of fish to cook and eat. With fruits that I had stored in my bag when I hurriedly prepared to leave, we had a most wonderful meal by the fire, the wind blowing through the windows from the ocean breeze.

Gaspar thought of everything. Pulling out the book, Gulliver's Travels, he began to read. I interrupted him and asked why he hadn't asked me to bring the Bible, and he replied that he didn't want to endanger the only Bible that I had from my mama'. The answer brought tears to my eyes. This pirate cared more for me than anyone ever had.

A while later, Gaspar noticed my head nodding. I couldn't fathom the reason that I could not stay awake. After such a remarkable day, I expected to be too excited to sleep. As he stood to take my leave and go outside to the small place he had made a bed, I rose to walk him to the door.

I didn't know what to say, so I laid my hand on his arm and looked up into those warm eyes. 'Thank you,' I whispered. We stood there for just a moment, and then he bent his head to mine, touching my lips with his, ever so softly. I reached up to pull his head closer, but he gently wrapped his fingers in mine and looked into my eyes. 'No,' he said to me. 'You are this man's salvation. Love cannot survive without you. Our time is not yet, but will be. My precious Magdalena.'

I stared at him as he pulled the door closed. Then just as softly, he opened it again. 'Monk told me that before I regained my senses and was ill, you came by every day to minister to me. He called you 'that Maddie girl.' I assume he didn't know your real name. In my mind, you have been my Maddie girl. Goodnight Maddie. I'll wake you before the sunrise.' And he smiled and closed the door.

I admit I slept my very best sleep last night. This morning, Gaspar was true to his word, yelling at me to wake up and see the sunrise. It was still dark outside as we made our way down a short path to the beach. The moon was still visible in the sky, but the brilliant hues of the sunrise made the stars disappear and the moon fade. Such blues and pinks I have never seen in one place. The birds were singing. You could imagine a choir of angels singing God's praises. The warmth spread through me as I watched that incredible orb rise and bathe the waters with colors, the air rich in clean, salty air. I turned to look at Gaspar, and he was staring at me. 'Yes,' he said to me. 'That is the look I wanted.' He put his arm around me, and we stood there until the sun had left the horizon for heights above the birds. As we turned to go back, a large sea turtle was making its slow way to the ocean. 'She's laid eggs,' Gaspar said.

That turtle made the trip perfect.

November 15, 1819

The past few days have been quite busy. So busy that I haven't seen much of Gaspar, and have frankly wondered if he is avoiding my presence. He seemed attentive when we arrived back on Captiva, but immediately dispatched the first man he saw to find Monk for a report on what may have transpired while we were gone. Gaspar helped me step onto the beach from the canoe and then turned to pull the canoe towards the seagrass. I wasn't sure what was expected, so I simply told him that I enjoyed our trip and would see him at a later time. He looked back at me and smiled, nodding.

Since that time, I haven't been alone with him. We haven't read anything, although I have made my mornings available. I haven't questioned Father Jacob, for he knows of our trip and looks at me in a queer manner. I'm sure that I need to reassure him of my continued maidenhood, but feel somewhat angry at being misjudged. I suppose that many would think I was quite the brash vamp, disappearing with a man overnight. Appearances are everything, my mama` would say. I know she is right, but I am stubborn. One of my many failings, I am sure.

I find myself reaching up to touch my lips, remembering the soft touch of his mouth to mine. The memory sends a shiver up the middle of my back until I shudder and clear my head. Is this love? Having not found myself in this particular area of emotion before, I find myself needing guidance. And have not one idea on where to seek such counsel. I feel like a silly goose for looking for someone to confide in. I realized that I am already sixteen and several months old – an old maid, as my Padre said. I turned sixteen and didn't even know the day. No matter, it's only a year. It feels like a different lifetime ago. I will know the date I am to be 17. Only a few months away.

I will talk to Father Jacob tomorrow.

20 November 1819

Father Jacob and I traveled by canoe today, only around the end of the island, and then turned and returned. I am to be taught the ways of rowing and using the oar to maneuver the little boat. Gaspar asked Father Jacob to instruct me, so that I may go where I please, but only with accompaniment. I inquired why I would need someone with me if I were to learn to do it alone, and Father Jacob only said that anyone in a canoe should know what to do.

I find it quite exhilarating to row myself around, even with Father Jacob supervising. The freedom to move from one place to another is a new one. Other than walking from one house to another, travel was always arranged by someone. I had been carted around, much like chattel. A daughter of a Spanish aristocrat certainly did not go anywhere unaccompanied and was not allowed to make decisions about traveling.

I have realized that this island has given me freedoms I would never have experienced in Spain, under my Padre's observant eye. My mama` was right. God does take bad things and use them to His will. I have been fortunate and even blessed with the capture by these pirates. I know many have not, and it breaks my heart that many have suffered at the hands of these men that I walk with each day. How do I reconcile these feelings? How do I feel compassion and even love for these men that have been so violent? My heart, my very soul, is confused.

Even with the private time today with Father Jacob, I could not bring myself to talk about my feelings for Gaspar. I cannot reconcile my feelings for this pirate with my feelings of unease about his livelihood. He is a pirate, after all.

Father Jacob says that Gaspar has found God, for the second time, it seems. So why does he still steal from the merchant ships and take those things for his own? Father Jacob had no answer for me, saying that a leopard couldn't change its spots all at once. Such a strange saying. He said I should be very content that Gaspar is not hurting anyone, and has passed along that proclamation to all who follow him.

The evidence suggests that most of Gaspar's men are loyal to him, following his rules and bearing him no ill will that they are not allowed to use the women as they have in the past. Of course, Father Jacob may have planted a seed in their hearts, if they have one, of the power of God and His commandments. It's regrettable that "Thou shalt not steal" hasn't seemed to sink into these pirate's invisible souls.

Gaspar is not stingy with the bounty he collects, distributing everything equally, and taking very little for himself. He seems to take pleasure when it is a Spanish merchant ship and specifically one from the court where he was once a member. Gaspar obviously is still stung by the rejection of his lady in the court.

I have asked myself if Gaspar truly has feelings for me, or if I am simply a whim to take his mind off the woman he loved, and perhaps still does.

I must talk to Father Jacob. My confusion keeps me awake, and I find myself nodding in the middle of the day. If this is indeed love, I may not find a good use for it.

Tomorrow is December! I realized that I did not have the opportunity to celebrate mass last Christmas, and am thankful that Father Jacob is here to help us all celebrate this year. I want to plan an extra special day of thankfulness. I have been pleasantly surprised that most of the men, though pirates, do have an understanding of God and worship in a way unbeknownst to me. They know Psalms and sing hymns that I have heretofore unheard. The manner of their speaking goes into their song, but they have the right idea. It is a praise to our Lord.

Gaspar has been scarce as of late, taking a ship and traveling south to a country called Venezuela. I have heard of this place; it is trying to establish itself in this new world. I don't believe that it is quite as far along as this Florida has become. I have yet to travel the Florida mainland; I understand that it is quite close and easily navigated. There is a small settlement there. Gaspar and his men trade there and supply many of the families there with goods, as well as trading with the other native peoples that are on the mainland.

I look forward to meeting people that have traveled far to establish a new home.

December 21

It has been so long since I have written a word! Preparations for the Christmas mass have tired me, and I have fallen asleep immediately upon retiring, only to arise with a full day ahead. The chapel is beautiful with ferns and flowers adorning every possible background. Father Jacob has been preparing a most enjoyable talk and practiced it upon those of us bringing in the flowers and greenery. The small chapel is as pristine as possible and ready for our day of celebration of our Lord's birth and thankfulness for His grace.

The most advanced cooks among us are preparing an elaborate feast for everyone, and the aromas surrounding our settlement are delightful.

I had hoped that Gaspar would return in time for the mass, but there has been no sign of the ship. We did have a visitor from another boat assuring me that Gaspar had reached his destination, due to the Beacon of Maracaibo. When I responded that I didn't know of which he spoke, he only replied that Gaspar would fill me in.

December 25, 1819

A glorious day, indeed! I tire from all the food, and I am simply drained from singing and praising our Lord and welcoming His Birth. It has been to the point of perfection; I wish I did not yearn for the pirate's presence. That gift would have made the day my most memorable so far.

Later

I was interrupted in my recollections of the day by a knock at the door. Not wanting to wake Elena, I wrapped a blanket around my shoulders and stepped outside, thinking it was probably Father Jacob. Gaspar stood there, smiling and holding out a gift. The most beautiful bird I had ever seen. Sitting on his shoulder, he offered me the small rope he had tied to his leg.

I told him I didn't want to hurt him, and Gaspar assured me that I would not. Offering the bird my sleeved arm, the brilliantly colored bird hopped over and looked quizzically at me, tipping its head to one side. A parrot, I'm told, a macaw parrot. And Gaspar said that this bird talks which indeed it did! Quite clearly, the large bird repeated 'Maddie' after Gaspar, and then proceeded to bob its head up and down. It looked to be smiling, genuinely smiling! A bird. I was taken aback. Gaspar told me to give this bird a name. I didn't hesitate. Farris, I told him. After the pirate that had saved my life, and Gaspar's. Gaspar bowed to me and, without any further instruction, left. I had no idea what to do with Farris, but Farris seemed to have his own opinion and settled in the corner, atop the back of a chair. There was an old rug on the floor. I picked it up and hung it on the chair for any excrement that I was sure would appear. After placing a wooden bowl filled with water on the floor next to the chair, I returned to my bed, only to arise to write down the events of the past few minutes. Now I go to bed, hopefully, to sleep, but I fear that I may spend much of the night watching Farris, although he has tucked his head into his wing and appears to be sleeping. A most amazing gift on a most wonderful day.

As the new year approaches, I have much to be thankful for. Although I can't say with any certainty that Farris is one of them. This parrot does not want to leave my side or my shoulder, I should say. Always picking at my hair, I have to reprimand him repeatedly. He squawks and repeats 'Maddie, Maddie' until I can't help but laugh, which he has also picked up on. His laugh is hysterically comical. Elena finds him quite charming, which is a good thing, I suppose. It would be horrid if Elena wanted me to put the bird outside.

I do like the bird, of course. I sense that we will grow close with time. He does, however, require quite a measure of maintenance. Gaspar has assured me that he can be taught the niceties, as he had a parrot in the past.

Gaspar has told me of his adventures in Venezuela, where he procured Farris. The people of Venezuela are not particularly fond of Spanish and would refuse to allow a Spanish ship to enter their port. They are aware, however, that Gaspar has renounced his claim to Spain and works for himself. Trading with one that also feels loathing for the hierarchy of Spain is acceptable, and Gaspar and his Venezuela port friends trade merchandise often.

There are astonishing stories about the Beacon of Maracaibo. Such fantastic legends exist, who knows the truth or myth of them? Gaspar told me that he had heard the stories for many years about the beacon. Sailors and pirates alike talk about the lightning that warns them they are closing in on land and gives them direction during a storm. This beacon, as they call it, appears to be a mystical event in pirates' tales, as the lightning appears more frequently and sometimes nightly despite there being no storms brewing. Unrequited love and long-lost ships surround the myths that are told. I laughed as Gaspar told me of the beacon, and he studied me with such coolness in his eyes that I had to question his belief. He only said that there are things not of this world we cannot understand. Rubbish, I responded, and he smiled at me. That smile. The one that should bring those lips close to mine once again. But I was not to be rewarded. Father Jacob interrupted our conversation and asked for Gaspar to join him.

A new year. I have read some of my past entries and decided that I have become much too maudlin and not accurately factual for something meant to be read by my children and grandchildren, should I ever have any! I don't want to become macabre in my desire to save some small part of myself to pass along, but there is little else to pass along! I have no property, no grand name, or family inheritance. Indeed, I feel certain that my family has all but renounced me for my failure to respond to my fiancé's request.

I'm such a foozler, I am. The likelihood of anyone being around to read something thrown in the box with my bones is not probable. I can write what I like. If by happenstance someone does read it, they will read the ridiculous musings of an old maid left on an island with her parrot, Farris.

Father Jacob has asked that I help him brighten up the surroundings of our little community, such as it is. There are several families here now, with two babies on the way. It is quite heart-warming to see the pirates turn into men who adore their brides and rest loving eyes on the round protrusions carrying their offspring. Credit lies with Father Jacob in bringing about such beautiful and meaningful sermons to all who come and listen. I am sure that he has deliberately forgotten some of the requirements for mass, and likewise the requirements for entry into God's grace and communion, for all who come and kneel in the chapel receive Father Jacob's blessings and the Holy Communion offered by our Lord.

I do not doubt Father Jacob's love for our Lord. He prays often, and with tears of both joy and sorrow. I think he hears God's voice in his heart and follows the wisdom he gains from his prayers. To have such faith! I pray for that faith each day.

I also pray for Gaspar to kiss me again. I don't believe that God minds.

We have not seen many ships pass by, even looking far into the horizon. Gaspar says that there is trouble brewing in the sea, but he didn't elaborate.

January 15, 1820

Gaspar called for me today, sending Monk to request my presence, with my mama's Bible. I pointedly took small slow steps, following Monk to

Gaspar's cabin. I did not want to appear too eager to see Gaspar.

Gaspar had prepared – or more likely, had made by Elena, a delicious meal of perfectly cooked alligator and yams. Motioning for me to sit at the table with him, at a setting prepared for two, I placed the Bible to the side of my plate and looked at him with, I hoped, just a hint of a smile. I knew very little of the flirtations I had seen other girls display for men, but wanted to flirt, just the same. Oh, dear, what a disaster I am!

Offering me the alligator, I obliged by taking some of the meat and placing it on my plate, along with a helping of yams. As we ate, Gaspar told me of the trouble in the sea. Wars of independence were commonplace between the Spanish, the French, and the English with islands they had populated. There were rumblings of dissatisfaction with rule from lands far removed from the islands. Spain had ended the slave trade in all of the colonies, but Cuba retained its hold and continued slavery with help from the British empire.

I admit to little understanding of the lessons he was willing to teach and probably have misrepresented some of what he told me here. I was impressed with his passion for the subject and was content to listen to him talk and see the concern on his face as he understandably considered the fate of those on islands he had visited.

I was also confused. This man, this pirate, was exhibiting concern for others that were not a part of his clan. They were not pirates, but people on islands, unlike him, but people he had met and learned to both admire and respect.

I have no excuse for my actions. I arose from my seat while he was talking, wiped my mouth with the slightly faded napkin that had been laid at my plate, and walked around the table to Gaspar.

Gaspar had stopped talking and was looking at me with some alarm. Did he think I meant him harm? I almost laughed as I imagined any attempt by me to do so. Instead, I leaned down and pressed my lips to his, keeping my hands at my side.

Gaspar stood and looked at me, my eyes rising to his face as he towered above me. I couldn't tell if he was angry or not. He took a deep breath and pulled me close to him, letting his mouth find mine in a not quite so gentle manner as before. I could feel the muscles of his arms around my shoulders, the rise of his chest against mine. My hands found his neck, and I pulled myself up, closer to his face, to continue the kiss that I never knew I had desired.

I can feel it still, here in my room. My face grows hot with the thought of it. I was the one that broke off the embrace, not for any reason other than I could no longer breathe. I had placed my hand on his chest and pulled back, but he took my hand in his and let out a long breath.

Gaspar said one word. 'Maddie.' As I looked into his eyes, I saw something there that I wasn't sure I wanted to see. I was afraid to find out what it was. I left. I just turned and left, forgetting my mama's Bible lying there on the table.

There will be no sleep for me this night. I yearn to dream, but what if there are nightmares? Of what I do not know.

January 16, 1820

I did sleep. A deep, dreamless sleep. Perhaps preparing me for the day to come. It has not been fruitful.

I am usually the first one out of the cabin in the morning, but when I rose, Elena's bed was empty.

I continued my morning rituals and straightened both beds before I left. Even now, I read these words back and see that I have come to see so many things differently. What I would have rightly called a cot only a year ago has now become my bed — layered with beautiful quilts from where I do not know. Bounty from some merchant ship, I'm afraid. But I claim them as mine. I suppose that the very act of sleeping under these beautifully sewn pieces of cloth makes me a thief also. I will have to pray about this.

As I left our cabin, I found Elena sitting outside on the bench placed outside the door. She was staring out into the distance, a small smile on her lips. Noticing me, Elena moved over to allow me room to sit. I asked her how she came to be up earlier than usual, and she told me that Monk had knocked ever so softly just before dawn. She saw that I was sleeping soundly and left to walk with Monk on the beach and watch the sunrise. Monk had asked for her hand, and she had said yes. I had not known that their attraction has progressed to this point, and acting as a young girl, I asked if they had kissed. I was quite curious as to her reaction to this physical action, the one that caused such ripples along my spine.

Elena seemed to be surprised that I would ask such a thing. 'Just a quick peck is all,' she said, and her face turned quite pink. I am not sure that she was telling me the truth. Elena then surprised me. She asked if Gaspar and I had kissed. I was not aware that there was anyone on the island, save Father Jacob, that knew of my attraction to Gaspar.

'Everyone is aware of the mysterious glances between the two of you,' she told me. I feel so naïve.

As I gathered my wits about me, I asked Elena about her plans for marriage. She replied that she and Monk would talk again once he returned. With a sinking heart, I asked where he had gone. She said that Monk had taken Gaspar, leaving the island in the canoe. He had not known how long he would be gone but wanted her to understand his feelings for her before he left.

I have not been myself this day, scarcely remembering what else I have done to get to my bed once again. Elena is sleeping peacefully, but I cannot find rest. Father Jacob does not know where Gaspar has gone or when he will return.

February 20, 1820

I do not know what date it was we left the island, only that we returned a few days ago. Father Jacob roused Elena and me in the middle of the night, hours before the dawn, and rushed us to the lone canoe left on the island. Reaching for my journal, I realized I had left my mama's Bible in Gaspar's cabin. I would not be able to retrieve it. Wiping away tears, I grabbed my journal and placed it in my satchel along with my change of clothing, and placed Farris on my shoulder, but Father Jacob said I must let him go to the trees and hide. His shrill voice would give us away. I hesitated as we drew near to the small boat, and then gave Farris the okay to fly. As he flew to the trees surrounding our settlement, I suspected even Farris knew of the dangers coming. Elena and I climbed in as Father Jacob took the oars. Telling us to be very quiet, he rowed to the other side of Captiva, pulling in among reeds and tall grasses. He whispered that word had come that our village was to be raided, and he had done all he could to get everyone to safety. He had alerted everyone he could and then came for us, as he had promised Gaspar and Monk that he would. We sat in the small canoe and listened to the noises throughout the night, the sounds muffled because of the distance. But we could see the fires burning. I thought of my mama's Bible and Farris. We prayed for the others in our village, and we prayed for Gaspar and Monk. We once heard voices in the distance and remained quiet as the glowing red eyes of alligators passed beside us. I held Elena's hand and squeezed so hard I thought I might break her fingers as she trembled at the sight. I had not realized that we had pulled into a small brook from the ocean, the reeds concealing the edges of the swollen banks from the recent rains.

The sun had begun to rise high in the sky before Father Jacob felt it safe enough to venture back from the direction we had come. Carefully and slowly maneuvering, staying concealed behind the beachgrass, Father Jacob brought us to a beach that was defiled with rubbish strewn about, bottles of every color broken and discarded. Birds were pecking at the spilled contents, mostly rums I assumed. It was as if the invaders had thrown a raucous party after they had burned down the other side of the island. I was anxious to get back to our village, but Father Jacob would not allow it. Following instructions from Gaspar, he bade us remain in the canoe as he pushed the small boat in the stream to the ocean. He rowed toward the mainland seen in the distance. As we rowed out in the calm waters, we were met by another canoe that frightened both Elena and me, but Father Jacob appeared undisturbed by the visitors. The two men in the canoe did not speak but slightly nodded at Father Jacob, pointing toward a small rill opening up onto the water from the mainland. The men were clearly natives, having very little clothing and brown as the dark rice we boiled over the fire. With kind eyes and dark braids, I bade them 'thank you' as we rowed toward the safety of the mainland.

Upon our arrival, Elena and I stepped gingerly on the moist soil of the mainland, surprised that we had entered a proper settlement, with small buildings and people walking the makeshift street. I supposed the banks of this river was an appropriate place for trading. The river was called Caloosahatchee by the natives, and it seemed appropriate there were different peoples congregated there. Besides the occasional native, I recognized peoples from countries other than Spain and England, although my homeland and England were represented. There was also a petite gentleman selling beautiful tapestries from a country unknown to me, with dark slanted eyes and a long braid hanging down his back. Father Jacob explained that very few people really lived here, but traveled here for trading, selling, and buying all kinds of merchandise.

Elena and I were targeted as merchandise, as Father Jacob had to tell more than one rough-looking man that we were already spoken for by the pirate Gaspar. The very mention of Gaspar's name tended to halt any type of bargaining they were attempting. I came to realize that many of these men were pirates themselves.

Father Jacob hurried us along to a large cabin at the end of a long row of wagons and horses. Knocking on the door, an attractive woman opened the door and welcomed us into a well-kept room. An older man sat at a table and, upon our arrival, put down his quill and placed the paper he was writing on inside a pouch he had on the table. He called us 'Ladies' and asked that we sit. He said his name was William Wirt, and that he served at the pleasure of President James Monroe, the president of this America, this United States. He also said that Florida would one day soon be a part of the United States of America! I found this quite surprising because my homeland of Spain has laid claim to this land, rough and uncivilized as it may be. I, of course, did not correct him. I confess that a certain part of me admired the people of this new *world in their desire to appropriate this land for themselves. They were the ones working to civilize it, were they not? But I remembered that Gaspar had told me stories of the natives of this wilderness called America. How many of the natives, living here long before anyone came from our world, were being subjected to horrible conditions and revolted against incoming invaders. Gaspar led me to understand more about our wrongs in coming to this country than I had ever contemplated and also bears more discussion and thinking.*

As I said, I did not defend my native Spain as the proprietor of this Florida. Mr. Wirt was very respectful and polite to us. I certainly did not want to discourage his attitude.

It appears that Gaspar had done this gentleman some service in the past, and it was Mr. Wirt's duty to protect us until he had ascertained that it was safe to return to our village on the island.

This was a long process. We were given a small room in a building that was adjacent to Mr. Wirt's, although we did not see him again after that first visit. Father Jacob was in a room across a small hallway from us, and in these rooms we spent much of our hours during the excessively long time we were there. Father Jacob did find me a copy of

Jane Austen's new book, "Emma," and I read aloud to Elena until my throat grew sore. Father Jacob also found a tattered Bible, but it was a blessing nonetheless, as we all prayed daily for the safety of others in our village, and the safe return of Monk and Gaspar. Bible passages helped me to reclaim my stability, as God himself promised. I read and reread His verse Psalm 46:1, 'God is our refuge and strength, an ever-present help in trouble.' The Psalms are ever comforting. If indeed, King David wrote the Psalm, it gives me hope that he, as a sinner, found his love of the Lord so inspiring that his trust remained with his Lord even as he was broken. I vowed that I would talk to Gaspar more about this when we next met. And I prayed we would meet again.

I had my journal with me but did not write for the duration of my stay on the mainland. I was always accompanied by someone and never alone. My writings are done in the quiet of my own contemplations. I did not want conversation surrounding my writing and did not want to give any explanations of what I was writing. Strange, is it not? I do not want to share what I have written with anyone, yet guard this journal so meticulously? Perhaps someday, long after I am gone. If there is anyone left that would be in the slightest interested *in the ramblings of an old maid that decided to remain in the New World against the wishes of her father and mother, and the old man that she had been promised to marry.*

I am becoming maudlin, am I not?

I have not yet seen Gaspar, though we have been back in our shattered village for a few days. Spending all of our time righting the mess we found when we returned, I have had little time to dwell on his absence. There were a few buildings and cabins left, although most were burned, the belongings thrown into a fire in the middle of the settlement.

The dead carcass of the large cat-like animal I had been feeding was the catalyst for my complete release of tears and wails of pain and fear. There were bird feathers near the carcass, and I imagined that they belonged to Farris, although there was little else to suggest so. I do not know why seeing this animal lying dead at my feet and feathers from a bird, even should it be my bird, would break open my heart so. I fell to my knees and screamed at the sky, quieting the sounds of birds and insects. The few others picking through the remains stopped, staring as I ranted and beat the ground with my hands. My tears wet the ground and dropped undisturbed onto my smock. Elena pulled me to my feet after I had nothing left to expunge and held me as my sobs dwindled.

Father Jacob said that there must be something to break open the shell that had held my fears and angst these past few weeks. The pitiful remains of an animal I barely glimpsed broke the shell. I have not yet seen Farris, but have hope that he will return when he hears my voice. I pray I have not just seen his remains.

February 24, 1820

We have made makeshift cabins for those of us that have returned. Word reached us that several in our village have decided to remain on the mainland in another settlement further down the coast. Belle and Antonio, along with Sophia, have agreed to stay on the mainland. There is a midwife close by, and Belle is full with child now. I will miss them and had looked forward to being involved in the baby's first few moments. What a glorious thing that must be.

I knew that Gaspar was on the island when Elena yelled out with joy and ran towards the edge of the clearing to welcome Monk back. The huge pirate picked her up and spun her around, her laughter infecting everyone around. 'Are you ready to get yourself married, now, woman?' he had teased her. I looked around, hoping to see Gaspar and realized that he wasn't with Monk. I had turned to go back to our work when I looked up and saw him parting the brush on the other side of the clearing, entering with Farris on his shoulder. Not restraining myself, I ran to him and put my arms around his neck, burying my face in his chest. I didn't realize how scared I was that something had happened to him. He had a limp, I noticed as I was heading to him, but he was here. Gaspar was here. And he had Farris with him. The parrot jumped on the top of my head shouting 'Maddie! Maddie!'

I stepped away and wiped my sleeve across my eyes. Tears had come from nowhere and streamed down my face, while laughter escaped from my throat. I'm sure I was quite a spectacle.

Gaspar looked down at me, taking Farris from my head and placing him on Father Jacob's shoulder, who had appeared at his side. He ignored Father Jacob's questions and took me in his arms. That kiss was the one that told me I had his heart, as he had mine. All else could be overcome; we would be one. The kiss for all to see, our souls laid bare; the tenderness and possession that would bind us together. The pirate was mine, all the good of him and all the bad. I was his, all the good of me and all the bad.

Gaspar looked down at me as we caught our breath. 'Marry me,' he breathed. I could only nod my head. I can barely remember the next few minutes. Gaspar said we would talk again in the morn; I feel I won't sleep again until I see him. Elena is sleeping soundly in the cot next to me. Farris is on his perch, swaying precariously, although he seems to have a perfect balance. My love is back. My doubts are gone. Prayers thanking God for grace, and Gaspar's return are ongoing. Many more will go as I pray for guidance in the days ahead. I feel guilty asking for more. God has answered and showered me with hope and love. I have no doubts that I have His blessing for my marriage to Gaspar. My heart could not sing; my soul could not rejoice if it were not true. God has shown the right and wrong of things. I have only to look to his Word. His grace. His forgiveness. His promise of new life. My cup runneth over.

February 26, 1820

I missed writing last night, my heart was full, and I was so sleepy my dreams began as soon as my head touched the down pillow. The past two days have been a whirlwind of activity for the few of us that remain here. Monk and Elena are to be married tomorrow. Although I would have been willing and ready to be married to Gaspar during the same ceremony, Gaspar said we must wait a few more days. He insists that we wait until the Angelinia, Gaspar's flagship, arrives from Spain. I asked what was on the ship, and he only smiled with that mysterious expression I have come to love.

We have talked; we have talked for hours. Gaspar is genuinely a man of the sea, riding one wave of happiness tempered with the next wave of despair and angst. Joy for our love, and guilt for the life he has led before. He has no regrets for leaving his homeland and his family. He felt their betrayal deeply. I am not aware of the events surrounding his departure, aside from his misguided trust in Rosalia. But he has deep regrets for his actions since that time. Not a man to cause pain to another, and not one with a taste for murder, he nevertheless knew that the men, the pirates under his flag were committing atrocities that he ignored. He felt, rightly so, responsible for their actions. I find I can love a person deeply, and accept the sinner and still love. For are not we all sinners? I cannot beg forgiveness and withhold it for another that also desires it. The desire for forgiveness I see in my beloved, this sorrow for the pain he has wrought is certainly enough for me, and it is not for me to judge at all! Only my Lord is the Judge. Our God sees all, His love abideth no matter the evil that sin stains us. His love washes it away.

I told these things to Gaspar, and he is not convinced, but his eyes hold out for hope, I can see it. We have read scripture, I have shown him the words that our Lord spoke.

Gaspar gave me my mama's Bible back to me yesterday. I had left it with him before we had left the island and thought it lost forever. When we returned to the island and found the burned belongings lying in the center of our settlement, I was sure that my mama's Bible was in the ashes. I questioned Gaspar how it was he came to have it.

Gaspar came to the village, missing us by only a few minutes as Father Jacob rowed us away from the beach. Although he could see us from the walkway to the beach, he dared not yell out for fear that the raiders would find him or try to follow us.

Gaspar had run through the village, checking that everyone was gone and seeing the Bible lying on his table, picked it up, and put it in his pack. I left the Bible when I rushed out of his cabin in embarrassment before he left the island; he thought I would return the next day to retrieve it. He knew he was leaving and would not see me for several days. He left me a note stuck inside the first page. As I read the note he had left for me to find, I'm sure I blushed. What should have been read privately I was reading in front of him! A love letter. I have placed it in the Bible where it shall remain.

February 28, 1820

Elena and Monk married and left for the mainland. They expect to return, but I am not sure they will. The continent offers much more opportunity and entertainment. I find myself appreciating the emptiness of the island. I love my friends, but the sounds of the breaking waves, the bird cries, and the whisper of wind-swept trees fill my soul with contentment. Farris, though a parrot, is my constant companion, and I can feel his content as we walk along the beach. He likes to perch on my shoulder, but he is also content to watch me from the trees bordering the seagrass. It is quiet here now. Gaspar says that the danger is past, the British navy had captured an old pirate nemesis named Grange. Grange had led the attack on our island, meaning to destroy his competition for pirating merchant ships in the area.

Grange was not aware that Gaspar had curtailed his trading in the area to only aiding the natives in their transport and bartering goods made or grown by their tribes. I was not fully aware of Gaspar's expertise in trade until he tried, with some patience, to explain it to me.

The natives around this vast sea have expertise in many areas, including growing delectable fruits and vegetables in this warm climate. The abilities of both the men and women of the tribes are skillful at beautiful furs and leathers from the hides of the animals they eat. Gaspar has befriended many of these natives and helped them to barter and trade to their advantage. This act brought him not only a reputation for goodwill among the native population but also thanks in the way of goods and produce. Now I finally know how we come to have such delicious meals!

Gaspar told me that the Angelinia should arrive within days. I continue to help Father Jacob repair the chapel. He is confident that others will return, and we will need the chapel for future gatherings.

March 5, 1820

The Angelinia sailed by this morning. I expected her to anchor within sight, but she sailed around the edge of the island from view. Gaspar left in the canoe to meet with her on the other side. He forbade me to come after him, hinting at a surprise for later. Not expecting him to return this day, I found Father Jacob and asked a favor. I have no need for an elaborate wedding or a feast, but I do desire to have a dress that is somewhat special for the occasion. Father Jacob seemed quite excited that I had asked for his help, and said that he was sure we could find something that would work with the splendid aplomb it should.

We spent hours going through the merchant trunks that have arrived in the past few weeks since the attack. Supplies from the mainland, as well as materials and household items, were sent in response to Gaspar's request after the raid.

Maria, a quiet, tiny woman that has been on the island longer than I, was helping go through the trunks when she came upon a beautiful piece of cloth, brilliant blue like the sea. She called me 'Mademoiselle,' which I quickly corrected to 'Maddie, please!' and said she would be happy to make a dress of the beautiful fabric. I had not thought of how I would have the dress made, and this was a gratifying, and once again, thankful event. Maria measured me from bosom to heel, and we decided upon a simple, flowing, ankle-length dress with a high waist and straps over the shoulders. Completely out of character with what high fashion would require in Spain or England, but I am a New World person now. I loved the way the soft, flowing materials felt against my skin and imagined it blowing in the winds from the sea. I begged Maria to allow me to observe her work, and she was embarrassed at my exhilaration of her expertise. The dress, in a few short hours, is almost complete. She has assured me it will be ready to wear on the morrow. Now I am truly excited. Just the thought of Gaspar's touch leaves me breathless. We have kissed once again, but not with the abandonment of the night he returned. I feel that he is holding back on his affections. I mentioned this to Maria, and she giggled nervously. I am beginning to think that there is something quite remarkable about the wedding night, above what my mama has told me and what I have overheard from the women in the village. If this joining of our bodies is in any way akin to the kiss, I scarce can hope to survive it.

March 7, 1820

I am ready to be wed, yet where is Gaspar? He has not yet returned, and although Father Jacob has assured me he will indeed come back, I have decided I will go to the other side of the island to look for him when the sun rises again.

March 8, 1820

The morning sun did not bring Gaspar, but Elena and Monk arrived, relating that they were invited to the wedding. Belle, Antonio, and Sofia arrived shortly after that, carrying their newborn, and another ship arrived with more wedding guests. I asked when this wedding was to take place, but no one knew the day or time, only to come and be prepared to stay overnight. I was beginning to doubt my sanity when Gaspar finally rowed ashore. Meeting him as he pulled the canoe from the water and turned to me, I stood with my hands on my hips, glaring at him, although I couldn't help but let a smile breakthrough. This roguishly handsome pirate was mine. I was his. The vows are essential. They are important for us, our friends, and promises to God. However, I know that our hearts are joined, as God will join us together in all things soon. 'Tomorrow,' my beloved said to me.

Tomorrow I will begin my life with Gaspar, as his wife.

March 16, 1820

I have read over the past few entries in my journal as I prepare to add to it. I am wed, we are wed, we are married! I am officially Magdalena de le Castille Gasparilla. Such a long name! I am, to myself, and this new America, Maddie Gasparilla, to my husband, Jose Gasparilla, my Gaspar.

My dress was all that I dreamt it to be, flowing and almost sheer. We did not wed in the chapel, as planned, but chose the last minute to walk to the beach, among the sand and the small waves breaking at our feet. Sophia had woven flowers for a tiara on my head, and I felt, for the first time in my life, beautiful. Seeing the love in Gaspar's eyes made me feel beautiful. Our friends surrounded us among the bird cries. Farris perched upon Father Jacob's shoulder as if overseeing the ceremony. 'Amen' is Farris' new favorite word, which is an excellent word to repeat. Some others have been questionable, but I have learned to refrain from trying to hush the parrot. To do so makes him more determined to speak louder.

Father Jacob was very solemn throughout the ceremony, but once it was over, his jubilance was evident. He told me many times how happy he was for both of us. I motioned for Monk not to refill his glass with more wine. Father Jacob did not drink often, and it was apparent he had reached his fill.

I thought that we would retire to Gaspar's cabin as night fell, but that was not to be. We had a moonlit canoe ride around to the other side of Sanibel on the calmest of seas. It was as if the creatures of the ocean and the water itself knew that this was a special moment. The moonlight behind Gaspar's head as he rowed. The look in his eyes as he gazed at me, making me feel cherished and loved. The little knot in my stomach on what was to come. I admit to a bit of fear, but not of Gaspar. No, never of my husband. But of my own body. Would my body do what it was supposed to do? I realized how incredibly naïve I was. I was to be seventeen years of age on my next birthday and knew next to nothing on the ways of men and what the marriage bed would hold.

I remember these feelings now and smile. Of the secrets the marriage bed does contain. The completion of one another, the abandonment of self. The fulfillment of a promise made, a promise kept, and the hopes of nights to come. Soul to soul, with God's blessing. It is as it should be, between man and woman, wife and husband. One of God's gifts.

Gaspar picked me up and carried me from the canoe, and I did not complain. The pathway was rough and strewn with broken branches, but he seemed to know the trail well and traversed it quickly. Setting me down in a small clearing, my breath held at the sight. The cabin, our cabin. Our Sanibel cabin. He had worked and brought furnishings that he had made by the locals. This was the secret cargo. There were no panes in the windows; that would come later. The breaking of the waves on the beach reached our ears throughout the night.

April 11, 1820

Tomorrow I shall be seventeen. Gaspar laughs and calls me a baby. I had never thought to ask his age, and when I did, he questioned if it mattered. I assured him it did not. Gaspar is to be thirty years old in the fall! I acted quite astounded and inquired, should I get him a blanket? He laughingly chased me throughout our cottage. I have named our cottage 'Sea Winds.' The plentiful breezes that make their way through the open windows are invigorating. Gaspar has made me a sign and burnt the name into the wood proclaiming our home. The name 'Sea Winds' is above the small bench Gaspar made for me. I can sit and feel the breeze while I shake the sand from my feet. We are isolated here, and we both adore it. There are a few natives here on the island, but Gaspar says he believes that the few remaining here are the last of their once large tribe, most having fallen to yellow fever many years past. The Calusa, he calls them. I have only spied an older woman and two children who look to be very young. Gaspar says that they are friendly, but shy and will not come near the cabin unless requested.

We do have to travel back to Captiva regularly for supplies, and I am to have a party there tomorrow.

I am excited to see friends again, but Gaspar seems preoccupied. Perhaps he is planning a surprise for my birthday!

We spend our days walking over the island, searching out new trees and creatures. Farris is quite the guide, squawking whenever he finds something he thinks is appealing. Much of the time, it is of no consequence, but he puffs his feathers out and struts like he has discovered precious treasures! Usually, it is a small lizard he has spotted or one of the alligators that frequent the streams that crisscross the island. I found it quite astonishing that there was fresh water on the island, surrounded by all the salty water.

Collecting water and wood for cooking fires are daily chores, but easily carried out. Gaspar has only left me once and was only gone a few hours before his return. I know this will not last forever, but I am guarding our time together here alone as much as I dare. Gaspar's trade arrangements with local tribes and settlers make it necessary for him to travel from island to island. The danger in his travels frightens me, and I cling to him at night, praying that God will watch over him.

The pirate Gaspar also has other hazards in his wake. Both the Spanish and British have a price on his head. He understands this and yet tries to conduct civilized and honest trades with anyone that treats him likewise — my prayers for his safety multiply.

But I mustn't think on these things now. For tomorrow I am to be seventeen! And I am wed to Gaspar! My life is blessed beyond my most exuberant dream! I am content to spend each day here with my beloved, sharing in the beauty of God's world around us. We read Mama's Bible every day. We talk about what it means to each of us, sometimes agreeing, others not, but always grateful. We will acquire more books to read; both of us enjoy the written word and what better place to enjoy it than here in this paradise.

Tomorrow I am seventeen! And I am not an old maid!

June 1820

I am not sure of the date – I had forgotten to retrieve a calendar from Father Jacob when I was last on Captiva. But I know it is June, it has been several days since the last of May. Another baby has been born on Captiva! Father Jacob was correct, others have returned, and the settlement is rebuilding. I have mastered the canoe and can now make my way around the island. Gaspar tries to curtail my voyages, as he calls them, but I enjoy the trip. I only travel when the water and wind are calm, and he cautions me to stay within sight of the island at all times. I believe he thought that I would remain on Captiva while he was away, but I did not want to leave Sanibel for that long. I treasure my solitude at times. I do not stay on Sanibel for long periods alone, but enjoy a day or two of laze staring out at the ocean. On Captiva, there is always much to do. I am more than willing to help out, of course, but the sea calls me back.

I am ready for my Gaspar to return, he has been gone for many nights, and I long for his embrace. For his laughter and his teachings.

Gaspar is teaching me to speak the language of the natives here. We believe that only the old woman and two children remain, having seen none other. The woman has bowed her head and laughed at my attempt to communicate, but I am not deterred. Gaspar can talk with her, but the children only turn away. We are trading supplies for the pleasures of her garden. Hachi is her name. My pronunciation is not perfect, but Gaspar assures me she understands. The name means 'stream,' and with the many creeks running throughout the island of Sanibel, I know why she would have received the name. My goal is to have the children talk with me also and not shy away with giggles. They love Farris and laugh at his antics, and Farris loves the attention. He is quite the comedian, turning himself upside down and cackling. Hachi has asked Gaspar why it is that Farris remains close by and does not fly away. Never having had a parrot before, I did not understand that it was unusual. Gaspar talked to her in her native language, so I questioned him about it afterward. He told her that no one but Breathmaker could explain some things. Of course, I needed to know about this strange name.

Breathmaker is the Creator God of many tribes in Florida, and I suppose the Calusa Indians may have adopted the name. I have watched Farris closely since that time. He can leave whenever he likes. He always returns and makes his presence known. We are his family.

Gaspar has left twice before for a trading voyage since we married. I expected to travel with him, but he left me here. He refused my request to go with him because of what he called 'the dangers of the sea.' I must admit it was difficult to hold my tongue in response, and Gaspar could tell that I was not happy with his answer. I plan on changing his mind and as a last resort, insisting that I be allowed to accompany him on a few voyages that may lead us to a trading port that he considers safe.

Gaspar has brought me gifts and relishes my happiness as I open his bag. Two new books: 'Frankenstein' by Mary Shelley, is said to be a frightening portrayal of a mad doctor – I am reading it now only in the light of day! And 'Rip Van Winkle' by a Mr. Irving. Gaspar has that one with him now, and we will trade once he completes the book. The Bible we read together, with discussions that are sometimes heated when we disagree on what the meaning is. I have a picture in my head of Jesus watching us and laughing at our childishness. Prayers end our days together and apart, both of us knowing we are in each other's thoughts. God has indeed spread His blessings over us.

Gaspar brought games from his last journey. Checkers and backgammon. I don't know how to play either of them, but Gaspar has promised to teach me when he returns.

I have been busy, especially when I visit Captiva. My friends from the mainland visit Captiva often, *and I enjoy their company. Belle has become quite the seamstress. When we first arrived on Captiva and feared for our lives, we were desperate to master the art of cooking and sewing as well as many other duties we had never performed. Belle exhibited some talent with the needle at that time and has perfected the trade. She sews for monied men and women on the mainland; they seek her out for her astute eye for color and style.*

My dear friend has helped me sew a sash for Gaspar. The stitches are not perfect, I must say, but it is a rather beautiful sash, with the dark blues and purples that he wears so well. Around his neck or his waist, it will remind him of me wherever he is and hopefully bring him home to me sooner than later. Once home, I have another surprise for him. I like my windows open to the breeze, and as I was watching the wind catch bits of material on the posts where I had placed clothing to dry, I had an idea. My perfect dress for my marriage will not likely be worn again. Why should it sit unnoticed with such color as matches the sky and ocean? Gaspar will be pleased when he sees what I have created.

June 10, 1820

I brought a calendar from Captiva on my last visit. I will keep it with my journal so that I will know the date, especially for those important dates I want to remember!

Gaspar finally came home, waking me early this morning. To be truthful, Farris woke me with such squawking I had to rise to see what the fuss was about. Hachi's children, Taima, the little girl, and Nokosi, the boy, were laughing at Farris as he jumped from branch to branch on the tree outside the cabin. I opened the door and saw Gaspar standing there, poking at Farris' bright breast of color. Farris was quite enjoying the game and squawked, then jumped toward Gaspar wanting more. I think the parrot liked the laughter of the children.

Gaspar saw me standing there and smiled, placing a small bag on the ground and walked over to me. Pulling me close, I could smell the sweat of him, his damp hair clinging to his brow. Giggles from the children caused him to pull away and wink at them. I could understand a few of the words, as Gaspar pulled the bag open and handed me a gift he said was for Taima. The girl's eyes became wide as she

179

took it from my hands, and I motioned for her to unwrap the package — a beautiful wooden doll with meticulously painted hair and a perfect face. Taima hugged the doll and buried her head in her embrace. Nokosi put out a finger to touch the toy, amazed at its glaze and perfection, I suppose.

The next package was for Nokosi. Handing him the bag, Gaspar picked up the boy and sat him down on the ground, joining him as Nokosi opened the bag of white alabaster marbles. Showing the boy how to move the marbles around and the sound they made as they clacked against each other, Gaspar looked like a child himself.

After a few minutes of play, the children wanted to run and show Hachi, their grandmother. Gaspar nodded, and they looked to me. I smiled brightly at their attention; I felt they were becoming more comfortable with me. I nodded also, and they ran off.

Gaspar walked into the cabin and looked around in wonder. I hoped that was what the look on his face meant. His eyes did grow wide, and then he looked at me. 'Your dress?' he asked. The flowing lines of the beautiful cloth were blowing in the sea breeze. I told him that it only took a little help from Belle to make the cabin look like a wonderland of ocean and sky. I gave him his sash, which he placed around his waist and promised to wear always. It was a perfect homecoming.

Gaspar has gone to the creek to wash; I await his return.

September 11, 1820

I am so sorry, journal. I have been remiss in writing; so many other things to occupy my time and with the native children around so often when I am on Sanibel, I go to sleep quickly.

Gaspar is gone again, without me, although he did allow me to join him on a short trip to Las Martines. Such a glorious island! A friend of Gaspar's, Juan Pablo Salas, was granted this beautiful island a few years ago by the governor of Cuba for Salas' service to the crown. Gaspar and Juan were in the Spanish Navy together years ago and have remained friends. Juan and his family keep a home in St. Augustine but come to Las Martines often. It was grand to be able to talk to another woman and discuss things I have not even thought about in months. Juan's wife, Islamora, was fascinating and knowledgeable about this new country, this United

States of America. She also said many are calling their island 'Key West' because of its proximity to other islands and the mainland. I like that name. Key West. As a key to the western world.

For some inexplicable reason, this day, my mind is on this new world. The birth of a new nation must be full of perils and dangers. So many lessons to learn and rules and laws to be made. I realized that I must pray for this country, as I pray for my Spain. I pray that she will continue to grow and learn from mistakes made by those countries that came before. Tragedies will befall her, as they do to every country. My heart cries for those that will suffer and perish as they strive to make a better country.

But my sadness extends to those that were here before this country was born anew. Gaspar says some natives are forcibly moved from their homeland into unfamiliar territory. There are some invaders in this new land that favor war if it suits their purpose.

I read my Bible and try to make sense of it all. Gaspar says that God's Word says we must trust Him, that He is in charge. Gaspar speaks of the stories of history as if they were mere grains of sand. I had no response or argument with him as he spoke. His understanding of God's word surprises me. Gaspar says there is forever, and the forever means that we are to be with God. I want to believe; my faith in that would release me from sorrow and despair when I see the suffering around me. How much lighter would our load be if we truly knew that this was only for a moment in time? That our moments would be nothing compared to our eternity? Gaspar tells me to have faith. Faith in God's word. I am astonished at Gaspar's belief. He looked puzzled when I questioned him about his faith; it was such a short time ago that he was sure he was bound for hell. He told me, 'I have made peace with what I was, and yearn for God's path.' He pulled me into his arms and said to me that he thanked God every day that he had me. I feel so humbled. By God's grace, by His love, by His blessings.

Taima and Nokosi come around almost every day when I am on Sanibel. We are conversing slowly, and I get many laughs at my attempts at pronunciation. Hachi will accompany them occasionally, and I am trying to teach all three of them some of the King's English so that they will be able to converse with others that come. I fear that they will be using both Spanish and English in one conversation with me as their teacher! Taima means 'thunder,' and Hachi told me that she was *born during a big storm. Nokosi means 'bear,' and Hachi just laughed when Gaspar asked why he was named so. Taima is only four years old, but Nokosi is six. Both of their parents perished with the fever, and their grandmother was left to care for them. Hachi told Gaspar that there was one other on the island, a young boy older than Nokosi. Gaspar was concerned that he would bring harm to me, but Hachi assured him that he would not. The boy was scared of people; she claimed and had never spoken.*

I began to look around for the boy, but have not seen him. I have left food out that varies from what is readily available on the island. The food disappears, but I don't know whether it is to his hands or to another animal that has become adept at opening baskets. The basket is left in the same place, so I am hoping that it is the boy.

I have also been feeding another of the large cats I saw on Captiva. This one does not appear to be as large, and like the others, seems to prefer only meat. Gaspar warns me about the danger of feeding one of these 'panthers,' but I continue to leave out small bits for the cat with the yellow eyes. I have seen him watching me as I walk to the tree stump to place the scraps. Never having attempted to approach me, I nevertheless murmur to him as I slowly walk away.

I am sleepy now. It has been a long day, and I miss Gaspar. There is a storm approaching; the thunder is far away but not receding. The rain is refreshing, but a storm is troubling.

October 20, 1820

I waited in the early morning quiet for Gaspar's canoe to approach the beach. I could see his ship anchored and knew that he must be on his way. It seemed as if I had been holding my breath for weeks. Once I spied his ship in the distance, I felt a weight fall away from my breasts, and I could breathe again.

The storms had come, and although they quickly made their way across the island, the winds did destroy the pathways we had made, leaving fallen branches and hulls in their wake. My canoe was lost to the sea, even though I had tried to secure it.

Monk made his way to Sanibel within a few days to make sure of my safety. He reported that Captiva had also survived the storm; the damage was not as bad as the first storm we had endured. He tried to convince me to return to the mainland with him, *but I refused. I had to wait for Gaspar here. This is where he would come to me.*

Hachi joined me on the beach, looking out to sea for the canoe that would come around the edge of the island. She spoke to me, and I looked at her, not understanding. She smiled and placed her hand on my stomach. Nodding, she repeated what she had said previously. I looked at her, confused. She shook her head, trying to think of the words. 'Wee bebe?' she inquired. She patted my stomach again.

Finally, I understood. I shook my head, laughing. I told her no quite firmly, grinning at her quizzical look. She reached over again and patted my stomach. 'Bebe,' she said. Nodding, she reached up and put her arms around my shoulder and hugged me to her.

I'm sure Hachi thought me quite mad. I looked down at my stomach. It was protruding. I have always been slim, but now this little pouch. Of course, Gaspar had talked about this, and I admitted to him my lack of education concerning the ways of bearing children and rearing children. He had frankly told me that he was sure it would come to me. I admit to feeling a little nervous about the prospect.

The canoe appeared, and it was just minutes until Gaspar arrived. I resolved to talk to him about it later, and when Hachi walked off with a knowing look and a smile, I knew that I must speak to him soon. Could it be true? Am I with child? I haven't talked to my Gaspar yet, all this day we have walked, and he calmed my fears about the storm. He has left me to prepare our meal as he takes supplies over to Hachi. Farris was sitting on his shoulder as he strode through the trees, and I watched my beloved stroke the delicate feathers of our parrot. My heart jumped with the thought of a child. I must talk to him when he returns. I have no desire to eat.

December 1820

The weeks seem to crawl by. I am heavy and yet seem to have an energy level that requires me to constantly clean and prepare for the coming of our child. Gaspar only leaves for overnight ports, as he wants to be close as we rejoice at the life growing inside. I haven't been to Captiva in several weeks; I am content to stay here and watch the cabin expand to include a room for our child. Gaspar has been working and finding out the things that he cannot do, such as build a crib for the baby. Father

Jacob has thankfully agreed to procure a crib. Monk and Belle, along with their toddler and Sophia, often visit, bringing gifts she has made for the baby. I find this way of anticipation and joy at the prospect of a child much preferred to the English and formal Spanish styles. I would be shut away for the duration of my time, only to once again engage with others after birth. Gaspar has been so attentive and loves to touch my stomach and laughs with such joy when he feels the kick of our child.

I understand the meaning of the Psalm when David cries, 'My cup runneth over.' My cup, indeed, runneth over. Though this may only be a moment, it is a moment savored and cherished. As our child grows, our love ignites and burns ever so brilliantly.

The moments that God gives, these moments we must always be thankful for. My heart sings.

December 29, 1820

Christmas has been a glorious affair. Praise and adoration for the Baby Jesus are more meaningful to me now that there is another child on the way. I sit here alone now, stroking my large stomach, calming the life inside. The wee one is restless tonight.

Monk came earlier with news for Gaspar. I did not hear their conversation, but it required that Gaspar leave immediately. I could tell that he didn't want to go, he felt that my time might be close even though Hachi has assured him that it is still weeks away. Gaspar stood as I tied his sash around his waist and leaned over the significant obstacle between us to kiss me. As he held me close, the baby kicked, and Gaspar laughed and rubbed my stomach. 'Be well, little one,' he said. Looking at me with a loving smile, I assured him that the baby would not come while he was gone. 'My love,' he said to me. 'Make me no promises. God will have this baby come when He wills it.' Farris jumped to his shoulder as he turned to leave. Squawking, Gaspar stroked his bright feathers and told him to care for his mistress well. 'Amen,' Farris said, and we both laughed.

This moment. As I sit here, I want to hold onto this moment. My baby inside has quieted, resting. My beloved has bestowed upon me such blessings. Farris is in his corner, head buried in his wing, sleeping. As I look around our cottage, the sea wind blowing through the open windows, I am so thankful for this moment. All of these moments that make *up our life. Only a moment to God, a precious memory to me.*

January 1821

I am unable to breathe. I must breathe again, take a deep rush of air into my lungs, and fill my being with rational thought. I can't. Not now. How can I write?

I am alone. I told Monk to leave, and no, I told him I didn't want Belle to come.

Earlier this day, Monk walked up to the cottage on Sanibel as I was hanging clothing over the tree limbs to dry in the sun. I smiled as he approached, looking around him for Gaspar. Then I saw the sash in Monk's hand.

Gaspar had not allowed Monk to board his ship with him, asking him to stay behind. Monk had followed in the canoe when he saw the Navy warship over the horizon. Gaspar wanted to direct the incoming vessel away from Sanibel, away from Captiva, trying to protect our community and me. He alone would face the United States Navy with a price on his head. My Gaspar never had a chance to escape if there was ever thought of it. He could not avoid capture. As the men began to board his ship, Monk watched as Gaspar stood alone against the men, but was denied voice. He was wrapped in chains and thrown overboard.

His sash I hold and cannot let go. The smell of him is in the material; I cannot part from it.

Monk tried to comfort me, awkwardly holding me and patting my back. When I pulled away, spent from sobbing, he hung his head and apologized with tears running down his face. He was sorry he didn't save Gaspar, that he was too far away. Monk was also in pain, losing a man that was his friend. I tried to console him, but my mind couldn't grasp time or space. I told him to go back to Belle and let me be. I needed to be alone.

Farris knows. I do not understand how this bird knows, but he does. He sits on my shoulder, his beautiful crown of color resting on the top of my head, making no sound. His feathers quiver; he is grieving.

I will have to tell Hachi and the children. Another day. Another lifetime. I look down at my large belly and sigh.

Monk gave me a message from Gaspar when he handed him the sash, one to tell should he not return;

'Just a moment in time, God gives us forever when we meet again.

'

January 20, 1821

I sat this morning on the sand, looking out to sea. The ocean was a brilliant blue, with the sun rising just over the horizon. The colors were magnificent. I thought of spending an eternity looking at the waves rippling onto the shore.

I had to walk carefully over the sand and exquisite shells to return to the small rise with seagrass blowing in the fresh morning air. I feel so alone here. Although Hachi and the children are close by when needed, and my friends on Captiva will visit as often as I ask, I feel the loneliness without Gaspar deep in my very bones. I still crave the solitude, the time of visiting my memories and thoughts of our love. My pirate is gone, never to return, but in my dreams. And after this life.

As the morning broke over my Sanibel, the sun's rays warming the cascade of flowering vines and trees, I walked up to our cabin, our Sea Winds. I rubbed my hand across the bench he had made for me, felt his love in the smooth wood, and I prayed, as I pray each day. Each day prayers for strength, for endurance, but mostly for Gaspar's soul.

I will not; I cannot write again for a while. I must prepare for our baby. I am Maddie Gasparilla. This Sanibel is my home and will be my child's home. I can take care of myself and my child. I have been taught and loved by the pirate, Jose Gasparilla. I will not fail him nor our child. I feel the kick of our baby in my stomach, placing my hand there as I write this. Just a moment. A moment till eternity.

EIGHT

Lizzie closed the journal carefully, holding it on her lap as if it were a rare flower. Pulling a tissue from the box she had taken earlier from the kitchen counter, she wiped her eyes and stared out at the water. Deciding to finish the journal here on the beach was appropriate, she thought. The sun was setting behind her, the clouds over the horizon reflecting the pinks and purples from the rays. The same ocean Maddie watched, she thought. The same view as she waited for her Gaspar to return. The beach that Maddie's child played on. This is where her love, her Patch, came from. Where his heart and soul were grown, just as hers was born in the mountains.

Lizzie smiled at the thought. Could a beach boy and a mountain girl blend into a couple? A young, inexperienced girl from a respected family in Spain and a pirate managed to do just that.

Maddie didn't have the baggage I bring with me, Lizzie thought. And I don't have the courage that Maddie did, either. Maddie had faith. Can my faith be that strong? Can a young girl that was here on this island 150 years ago teach me how?

Lizzie looked down at the journal and said, "I want to try. If I don't, I'll always wonder if I gave up on living my life with the man I love so very much because I was scared to try."

Patch found Lizzie later that evening, asleep on the small couch in the cottage. Brushing the hair out of her face with his fingers, he whispered her name. Lazily opening her eyes, she smiled when she saw Patch staring down at her.

Patch started to speak, and Lizzie put her finger on his lips. "I finished it," she said softly. "Your great-something grandmother was incredibly brave. But I feel like I'm missing something. Is there more? What happened next?"

"We know some things, the stories that have passed down. We know the people born and the ones that died. Maddie had a son, Joseph. He married a girl from the mainland, and they had twin daughters. Rebecca and Isabella. Rebecca died, along with her mother, shortly after birth. Maddie helped with Isabella before she died. Bella, as is written in the letters, was a young woman when Maddie died, and received the journal from her. I have a few old letters that have survived. We'll go through all of those sometime soon. I can tell," Patch said, drawing his fingers across her face and the tracks of tears, "that it was meaningful to you."

"When did you read it?" Lizzie asked, curious as to how old he was, reading the journal of a young girl's innermost thoughts.

"Mom gave it to me when I returned from 'Nam. I heard a lot of stories about Maddie, about her trip here, her love for Gaspar. I knew a lot of it but had never read it from her journal. Her words, her handwriting, made it come alive for me. Along with you and my parents, her words saved me from the horrors of war. Our past and our present give us a purpose for the future. Once I was able to get past only looking inward, I could trust living again. Vietnam was such an ugly look at what people can do to people; I was afraid that I would never crawl out of that hole. Maddie's faith, your love, and my parents' prayers – that's what rescued me. I thought I had lost my faith."

Patch had been looking out the window as he spoke. Several birds were gathered around a small fountain, taking turns bathing in the rainwater. Patch looked down at her and took hold of her hand. "This journal helped to heal me. I was hoping it would do the same for you."

Lizzie sighed. "I know." Lizzie rose and walked to the window, looking up at his profile as he watched the birds.

Patch was silent, waiting for the answer he needed.

Lizzie grabbed his hands. "I need to go to my mountain. Before I go back to work, I need to go. There's something I have to do, and I want you to go with me. Please?"

Patch could never deny her. "Of course, we'll leave tomorrow."

"No, we'll spend another day here with your parents. I know they want to have you here at least another day. The next day?" She looked up at him, a question in her eyes.

"Okay. I'll ride back with you?" Patch had flown down to visit, knowing that Lizzie would be driving her 'Bug.

"That's perfect. Then we can drop off my car and pick up your Jeep. I need to go to the top. The Jeep will take it better." Lizzie stood from the couch and stretched.

"To the top?" Patch looked at her with a grin.

"To the Dome, you know, Clingman's Dome. I took you there before!"

"Oh, yes, I remember. All three million and fourteen steps." Patch put his hand on his wrist, checking his pulse.

"Silly!" Lizzie said as she lightly punched him in the arm. "You can make it!" Lizzie turned and headed towards the door. "I want to go walk on the beach. Oh, and by the way, I want a parrot."

NINE

John Oliver walked into the kitchen where Lizzie's mother, Beth Oliver, was packing up the last of the food to take back with them. It was always bittersweet to leave this place. They all loved it, but it was much too far to commute to his office in north Knoxville. They spent as many weekends as they could on the mountain, but other obligations at church and work prevented it.

Beth's parents had built the log cabin before she was born and named it Beth's Blessing. Beth had been her great-great grandmother's name, and it had been passed down each generation to a new girl born in the family.

Townsend, Tennessee, had been just a sleepy mountain town until a few years ago. Outside of Pigeon Forge, which was turning into much more than just the stopping point before Gatlinburg, more and more people had found the quaint and beautiful silence of Townsend the destination of choice. More cabins were going up.

Beth didn't like the change. She was afraid that she would look back one day, and it would not resemble the isolated, quiet setting she often craved.

John Oliver walked up behind his wife and leaned into her neck, kissing it softly. "Finished, my love? Are you ready for me to load the truck?"

Beth turned to him and nodded. "I suppose. Are you sure we shouldn't wait on Lizzie? They will be here tomorrow; shouldn't we stay and chaperone or something?"

Her husband laughed and put his arms around her. "My darling, always the worrywart. I think our daughter is an adult now if I'm not mistaken. She can certainly take care of herself. I'm supposed to be the one that worries about his daughter's virtue! And I'm not worried. Our Lizzie is a wonderful, successful adult, Beth, just what we have prayed for all these years." John's voice changed as he looked down at his wife, taking on a serious tone. "Lizzie had a rough time; she wants to put it behind her. We need to do the same for her sake. She is a Christian; she wants to do what God wants; what more could we ask?"

"But she gets so quiet and sad sometimes, John. And I know that I play a part in that. I pushed her. I might have been wrong; I probably was wrong, but..." she paused as her husband shook his head, "but I thought I knew what was best. I know we have to trust God; I know that she is trying to put aside the past. I trust her, I do! I can't help it; I worry. And you know, I think that Patch is the one for her. I'm not sure she knows it, and I wasn't sure myself, but now..." Beth looked up into her husband's eyes and saw the understanding there. "You're right. I think she has enjoyed her time at Patch's home in Florida. Now I guess she wants to share this one with him. You know she is going to want to introduce him to Sheba."

"Well, let's hope that it's not up close and personal," John said. "Now you've made me worry." He shook his head and looked out the window.

Beth turned and looked at him, smiling. "I know. Remember that our Lizzie is smart, John. She knows better than to get too close to a bear, any bear! She's been in these woods since she was a toddler herself. We've taught her well, sweetheart. I understand, I do! I watch them out the window, and it does seem like the bear is listening to her. The mountains protect, John. You simply have to respect them."

"You've told me that a thousand times, it doesn't make me feel any easier when there's a fire in the distance or bears protecting their cubs," he replied, looking into her eyes, the same eyes passed down to Lizzie. So dark, with light brown sparks flashing surprisingly with a smile.

Had to be the Cherokee in the DNA, he thought. He had never seen eyes like Beth's before he met her. One look and he was smitten forever. "I like that boy, well, I guess maybe a man. Patch is good for Lizzie. Maybe Patch can talk some sense into her. I doubt he will want to venture close to a bear."

"And neither will Lizzie, John! She doesn't go up and pet Sheba, for gosh sakes." Beth Oliver swatted her husband on the shoulder and turned to the counter. "Here, take these to the truck," she said, handing him two boxes.

As her husband walked out the front door of the cabin, Beth went to the door leading to the deck. Walking into the brisk morning air, she scanned the woods surrounding the cabin. Rabbits were hopping around, and birds were flitting between the trees, but Sheba was not showing herself if she was around.

Disappointed, she turned to go back inside when she heard the rustling of branches to her right. She leaned over the railing and spotted the black bear lumbering through the brush.

Sheba had first appeared a few years ago as a young cub, following its mother. Beth's daughter, Lizzie, had spotted the small bear in a tree several feet away from the outside deck railing. The two had stared at each other, both fearful, until the sound of a bear's growl alerted the young cub to climb down the tree. The cub scurried down the tree and joined her mother, taking one last look up at the young girl watching from the deck railing. The next two weeks found the mother bear and her cub arriving early in the morning and eating berries. Lizzie had asked her father if the baby cub was hurt. Between the ears on the small bear's head, a shock of yellowish-brown hair burst from the rest of the black hair. Her father had reassured her that although uncommon, black bears could have another color, including light brown and cinnamon. Lizzie knew this bear was special and named her Sheba from a Bible story she had read in Sunday School.

The next time her family was at the cabin, Sheba came again. And each time after that. Last year Sheba had come with two cubs of her own. Always mindful not to get too close to the bear or her cubs, Lizzie nevertheless talked to Sheba as if they were old friends. The bear had become satisfied that Lizzie or her parents would not venture from the deck and made use of the abundant berries within view of the cabin.

This crisp fall morning, Beth watched as the big black bear slowly moved to the largest tree. Amid the brush and other smaller trees, Sheba stood on her hind legs to scratch her back against the bark. After a few minutes, Sheba fell forward, landing on her large front paws, and walked over to the berry vines winding up the pine tree. Wild strawberries, Sheba loved them.

"Sheba," Beth said, haltingly. She knew that Lizzie talked to this bear as if she was her best friend, but it felt strange just the same. "Sheba, my daughter is coming up to the cabin. I think she wants to see you, and maybe introduce you to her boyfriend." Beth stopped and watched the bear as it continued to pull the berries from the vine and shove them into her mouth. "Long ago, I asked your spirit to watch over my girl and protect her. I know that's probably silly, but my grandmother wouldn't think so. Listen to my

Lizzie, Sheba. Give her your blessing." Beth turned to go inside and then twisted back again. "And don't you hurt my baby!" Her breath caught as she saw Sheba stop and look wisely at her, her large eyes boring into hers. Sheba shook her head from side to side as if to say that Beth had offended her. The large black bear turned and walked through the trees leading up the mountain.

A few minutes later, John Oliver backed out of the small driveway, then turned the wheels towards the gravel road that would wind down the mountain. Looking over at his wife, he prodded, "Why so quiet? Everything okay?"

"Sure. You know, just bittersweet leaving the cabin, like every time!" Beth looked over at her husband of 30 years and smiled.

"I know, and I'm sorry. But I do need to get back to work – you know, bringing home the bacon and all that stuff." John Oliver grinned as his wife playfully punched his arm.

"I think you may have brought home too much bacon," she said, pushing a finger into his side above his belt.

"I can still cut a rug if you want to," John said, laughing with her.

"Oh yes, we are big party animals. I would have to bring you home to put you to bed at 9:00. I think that dancing is out for us old folks."

Her husband looked at her with his eyebrows raised, laughing. "Who you calling old? Not me, I hope! And I wouldn't talk about going to bed. We can't even get through a whole episode of 'Marcus Welby' without you falling asleep. And that's your favorite show. I think you're in love with that young Doctor Kiley on there, what's his real name – James Brolin. Yeah, that's him."

"Hush! He doesn't have anything on you, sweetheart. Well, except for maybe for a few pounds around the waistline – he is missing that." Beth looked over at her husband with love. They were blessed.

TEN

Lizzie pointed to the cabin sitting amid pine trees. Patch had just rounded the most extended curve he had ever seen, going around and around, until he found himself at the top of a mountain.

"That's it. That's the cabin. Just pull over close to the door. We can unload there." Lizzie was ready to open the door before Patch had stopped and put the parking brake on due to the slight incline.

Lizzie grabbed the small bag and the grocery sack, walking up to the door with the key in her hand. "Come on!" she yelled back at Patch. Noticing he had not followed her after Lizzie laid the bags down, she walked back out to the Jeep. Patch was standing at the end of the graveled section, looking off into the woods.

Lizzie followed his gaze and smiled.

"I've never seen trees so beautiful," he said, his regard incredulous.

"You ain't seen nothing yet," Lizzie said as she grabbed him and pulled him away from the parking area. Walking him to the door opposite the entrance, leading to the deck on the back, Patch felt the breath catch in his throat at the view. The mountains piled one onto another, deep with reds and oranges, yellows peeking through. The sunlight touching each color, vibrating with the rustle of a light breeze. More green trees, firs, up toward the tops of the mountains, but the gradual descent into a myriad of rainbows was hypnotizing.

"I had not thought about it," Lizzie said. "We rode up to Clingman's Dome in the spring; you didn't get the best season for the mountains! We didn't come to the cabin. I'm sorry, Patch, but I'm kind of glad, too. I've shown you something from my home that you haven't seen before. Just like I saw at your cottage in Sanibel. The beauty of each."

Patch turned around and looked at the young woman he was bound to, with his heart. He nodded. "Yes, they are both beautiful. But not as beautiful as you." He took her face into his hands, looking into those brown eyes with flashes of gold. "Thank you."

"For what?" Lizzie asked as she put her hands over his.

"For bringing me here. I can see it means to you what the island means to me. It's a part of you; you take it with you wherever you go." Leaning down, he kissed her softly, then turned with his arm around her shoulders, taking in the glory presented in the sight of the mountains.

Lizzie turned to him as the wind rustled through the trees, giving her a slight chill. It was early for cooler weather, but the trees, draped in their coats of many colors, were always a reminder that snow-covered mountains were not far behind. "Come on in, let me show you Beth's Blessing."

"Beth's Blessing? Oh yes, right here above the door. What's that? A dove?" Patch reached up and ran his finger along the carving, a dove in flight, the name of the cabin burnt into the wood above.

"Yeah. My grandmother wanted to name the cabin 'The Dove's Nest,' but my grandfather convinced her otherwise. He wanted her name in it. There's a colored glass window with a picture of the same dove upstairs." Lizzie pulled at Patch's hand. "Come inside! It's cozy and quaint. Now don't make any snide remarks about it. I love this place."

Patch walked into a small entry with hooks hanging beside the door, and a mat on the floor. Shaking her jacket off, Lizzie threw the coat on one of the hooks and grabbed his hand again. Without walls separating the central area, the log cabin was small but just as Lizzie said, cozy and quaint. Exposed logs ran the length of the cabin, with a large stone fireplace in the far corner. The fireplace mantel, rich with picture frames, was made of the same wood as the logs. Patch wanted to look at each of the pictures, but later. To the immediate left was a kitchen, with clearly updated appliances and a beautiful stone counter. The main attraction to the room was undeniably the windows. Full-length windows covered the entire backside of the cabin, starting at the end of the kitchen counter and continuing to the stone fireplace. The deck was just outside, circling to the other side. The view Patch had witnessed outside continued here. He felt he was looking onto God's glory with the sight. Two rocking chairs and a swing were on the covered deck, but the roof didn't inhibit the view.

"There are two bedrooms down here; you take that one over there. Mine is over here. There's a full bath in each one. Kind of small, but it's enough. Upstairs," Lizzie pointed up the wooden steps rising from the floor between the bedrooms, "is the loft. There's a pull-out up there and a card table. Daddy says that someday he's going to get a television up there. But we don't get any kind of reception up here. You would think an antenna this high up would be a good thing, but...oh well. And there's downstairs, but you have to go outside to get there. Nothing down there but storage mostly. Hey, we've got music!" Lizzie pointed over to the stereo cabinet on the other side of the fireplace.

Patch nodded. "Yeah. This place is amazing. I love it. I could stay here almost forever, I think. But right now, heh, I just have to sit in those rocking chairs, please?"

Lizzie smiled, glad that he saw what she did. "Sure, let's go outside. There's someone I want you to meet."

"Outside? Oh, wait!" Patch grinned. "The real Sheba, right? Do I need to bring her something? Cookies or some other offering?"

"No, silly. You don't feed the bears. They have plenty to eat right here in the forest. That's why

Sheba comes close to the cabin; the berries growing right outside are like dessert for her. She probably won't be around now; I see her mostly early in the mornings." Lizzie unlocked the door to the outside; the breeze outside reminded her of the chill in the air. "Let's take a couple of blankets with us."

Stacked beside the door was a basket filled with rolled-up blankets. Each of them took one and pulled it around them as they sat and rocked, watching the birds jump from branch to branch, no clear destination but lots of chirping and communication with each other. There was no sighting of Sheba, the bear.

The afternoon fell into evening, and the twilight of the stars brought Lizzie and Patch inside. Groceries, mostly snack food, was put away. "I'm glad we have coffee. I'll have it ready when you get up tomorrow morning!"

"Right! Like you'll be up before me! I'll be the one fixing the coffee. Where are the coffee grounds?" Patch looked around the kitchen.

"In the cabinet above the toaster," Lizzie said, laughing. "So, I get to sleep in?"

"Sure! I can sit out on that deck and look around for hours." Patch said, pulling the coffee canister down from the cabinet.

"Come over here and sit by me," Lizzie said, patting the couch. The table facing the sofa looked as if it was a slice of a massive tree, glazed with shellac. The rings of the tree's life were easily visible. Lying on the table was an old wooden box. Lizzie opened it and began pulling out old photographs and notebooks.

"I asked Mom to get these out for me. I wasn't sure if they were here or at home in the city, but she said they were here in the safe downstairs. We have a large safe that's fireproof for obvious reasons." Lizzie stopped and looked off in the distance through the large glass windows. It had darkened outside, and little was visible except for a few lights down the mountain in other cabins. "We've watched the fires before with fear and sadness. So far, we've been fortunate, but there have been many who were not." Lizzie looked around the cabin. "This cabin is one of the oldest around here. Most of the cabins in this section are newer. My grandparents bought up twenty acres on this mountain back when it was cheap, so there's no one close by, but that means we're pretty vulnerable, too."

"I can see where wildfires would be terrible here, especially if it's been dry. What precautions do you take?" Patch asked, interested in how to protect oneself from a forest fire.

"A lot of it is education, educating other people about fires and not throwing out anything lit, like cigarettes or hot coals. Sparks cause some fires, you know, from lawnmowers. Even hot exhaust pipes on cars if you're driving over dry grass can start a fire. I worry about the animals. The wildlife can only go so far, and it's not like you can tell them not to go that way or this way. And there are lots of people that can't rebuild; either they didn't have the insurance that was needed, or maybe they didn't want to go through it again." Lizzie looked back down at the box, taking a deep breath.

Patch could see this was a hurtful subject. Picking up an old photograph book, he asked, "Who made these pictures?"

Lizzie smiled, realizing that Patch was directing her away from sad thoughts. "I think my grandmother made them; you can tell it wasn't a great camera, probably one of the first that came out!"

Patch laughed. "I don't think your grandmother was that old, Liz. The first camera was sometime in the early 1800s, I think. These pictures are..." Patch picked up one of the old faded photographs. "It's hard to tell what the picture is."

Lizzie leaned over and glanced at the small photograph Patch was holding. "I think that's a picture of one of the old Indian burial grounds. It's the one called Indian Grave Flats, I believe."

Patch put the picture down and looked at the stacks Lizzie was making. "What exactly is all this?" He picked up notebooks with pages filled out with notations and dates.

Lizzie put one set of papers down and looked at Patch. "This is part of my history, or what we have of it, anyway. Mom and I have been collecting everything we could find about our ancestors, and we've put it in this box. We've been through most of it and made sense of some of it. There are notes and stories, some old pictures, but none that go back to the oldest story we have, the one about Dustu."

"And Dustu is?" Patch asked

"Dustu is as far back as I can go in my history on my mother's side. He was a young Cherokee boy, hidden from the soldiers. His father was forcibly marched in what we now call the Trail of Tears to Oklahoma. We don't know whether he survived the trip or not. Probably not, since we haven't been able to locate anything about him. Dustu's father told him to hide, and then to go to a clan of Cherokee that was still in the mountains." Lizzie reached out and picked up another book. "I have lots of stories, but it's hard to piece it all together. Mom and I just haven't had the chance to keep looking. But for some reason, now it seems important. Maybe because

I read Magdalena's journal, I want to know more."

Patch asked, "What about your father?"

"On my father's side, I can go back several hundred years, thanks to old Bibles and letters. We've documented back to England and Ireland, along with some Scottish thrown in. Daddy said that his family brought the whole melting pot with him when they came. They did come early, in the late 1600s." Lizzie looked over at the bookcase in the corner. "We might have some of Dad's records here; it might be over there. It wasn't in the safe, so it could be at home."

"We can look at it another time. I think we have plenty to go through here! How about we try to put it in some kind of order, chronologically?" Patch picked up another stack of paper, stories written in different handwriting.

"Sounds like a good idea. I'll put on some hot chocolate and light the fire. Mom and Dad left us some firewood. It's not that cold outside this time of year, but it will be cool later. I don't have any heat on, but we can pile on blankets when we go to bed." Lizzie rose.

"Don't you want me to light the fire?" Patch asked.

"No, you sort through that stuff and make what sense you can out of it. All I have to do is light it; the firewood is ready."

Patch began sorting. He could tell by looking at some of the stories it would take some time to go through all of it. He didn't know how they were going to understand what was factual and what was possible. Shrugging to himself, he thought it didn't matter. They would be able to follow the general lineage, hopefully.

DUSTU

1838

Somewhere in the Smokey Mountains,
North Carolina

Dustu raised the branch hiding the entrance to the cave. He could see the tree line along the creek. A small bear was waddling through the water with a fish in its mouth. Dustu knew that the momma bear was close by; the bear was too small to be on its own. Probably the same cub he came across when he was looking for a place to hide and found the first cave. The little black ball of fur wanted to play with Dustu, but he retreated from the cave as quickly as possible and ran behind the trees. The momma bear was sure to be close; he didn't want to be inside the cave with both a momma and her cub.

Another cave, this one thankfully empty, was further down the mountain. It wasn't as deep, so bears probably wouldn't find it acceptable. Using branches cut from fallen trees, Dustu had made himself a bed in the back corner of the cave and laid rocks across the entrance with small pebbles lying on top. If the pebbles were disturbed, he would hear them. Fear had him sleeping lightly, if at all. He had counted four suns and four moons. Had there been enough time?

Dustu, which means 'Spring Frog' in the Cherokee language, was just shy of eleven years. He had not seen his father since the march of his tribe leaving the mountain. His father had pulled him aside and hid with him behind the high falling water. He had told him to run and hide in the mountain. 'Stay in the mountain,' he said, 'until all the soldiers and the march has left the Qualla.'

The Qualla is the Cherokee home, their land. Stretching over the mountains and valleys, bordered by the Ocona Luftee River on one side and lowlands spreading out on the other, the Cherokee people had made this their home for hundreds of years. The Ocona Luftee waters were sacred. Dustu knew that his ancestors had treated this river with respect. His father had told him the old stories about bravery and strength. The waters of their land purified them and made them strong Cherokee.

Dustu thought that the soldiers were gone. He did not understand why his father had to go with them to a faraway land, a place called Oak-la-home. Why could his father not stay here?

After the march, Dustu was to make his way to Chief Yonaguska. His father assured him that the Chief would take him in. 'Tell him the White Man Holland sent you there.'

Dustu did not know who this White Man Holland was. He had not met many of the white men. He did not like them. They spoke promises and did not act as they spoke.

Dustu watched as the small bear wandered off, and then he left the cave. He made his way down the mountain. He knew the way to the clan of Chief Yonaguska. Dustu must be brave and silent, like the wolf. He thought that the white man was gone, but there could be more looking for Cherokee.

Dustu went to Chief Yonaguska, and as his father had told him, Yonaguska took him in and treated him as his son. William Holland Thomas owned the land that Yonaguska called his own. Cherokee were not allowed to own property at that time, so Holland had the area in his name. Holland had been adopted by the Cherokee as a boy and felt compassion and kinship with them. He retained the ownership of the land until the United States changed the law and allowed the Cherokee to own it. The few Cherokee people that had been allowed to remain behind became the Eastern Cherokees, and the Cherokee people that made the horrible trip called the 'Trail of Tears' became the Western Cherokee.

Dustu never heard from his father again, nor from any of the clan of his father or mother. Chief Yonaguska told him that many had died on the trail, and they would be remembered by their sacrifice for the Cherokee Nation.

Dustu became a young man and a great hunter. He also never forgot his father and the lies told by the white man. Chief Yonaguska met with Holland often, but Dustu kept his distance when the white man was near. He did not want to talk with Holland, although Chief Yonaguska continued to tell him that Holland was a good man, even though he was not real Cherokee.

Dustu took a young woman from the clan of Chief Yonaguska as his wife. Her name was Salali, which means squirrel in Cherokee. She was quick to learn and openly adored Dustu. Salali had also lost relatives to the Trail of Tears. Dustu and Salali spoke of their love for their lost ones and consoled one another. The only disagreement between them involved the white man.

Missionaries were welcomed into the village by Chief Yonaguska and the white man Holland. Salali enjoyed listening to the white people talk of their God, ignoring the admonishment of her husband. Dustu told her that she should remain loyal to their gods and not look to the white man's God for sustenance.

Salali entered their small hut one day and tentatively asked Dustu to talk with her as she prepared the evening meal. Dustu had just returned from a hunt, and after cleaning himself in the nearby stream, was sharpening his spear. He agreed to listen to her concerns.

Salali told Dustu that she had two things she wanted to discuss. The first was that she was with child, and they would have a baby within the next few full moons. Dustu was happy to be a father and rose to go to his wife, but she stopped him. "Dustu, there is one other thing. I want to talk to you about God. Our Great Spirit and the white man's God. I believe that one is the other, and the other is one. I believe this to be true! Our Great Spirit, the Unahlahnauhi, means maker of all things to the white man. He is the God for all people. We may call Him the Great Spirit, the white man may call him God, but can He not be Unahlahnauhi for all peoples?"

Dustu was surprised but did not want to belittle his wife and the mother of his child. "I will think on this," he told her.

Time did not diminish Dustu's distrust of the white man and the white man's God. Salali continued to talk with Dustu, admonishing that there were clans that were not good Cherokee, just as there were white men that were not good white men. Explaining that there was good and evil in all tribes, white and red alike, did nothing to change Dustu's mind. However, Dustu did not interfere when Salali talked with their children about the Great Spirit and the white man's God.

Dustu and Salali had three children. Two girls, names Tayanita (meaning 'young beaver') and Yona (meaning 'bear'), came first. Both girls had reached ten years before their younger brother was born, Onacona ('white owl' in Cherokee).

Chief Yonaguska lived for eighty years, and Dustu was respectful of his friendship with the white man called Holland. However, when Chief Yonaguska died, Dustu did not want the white man to come to their village. He did not like that the white man wanted to be involved in the decisions of the clan. To Dustu's dismay, Holland brought his children to the village and made plans to keep them there, living in a house he had built on the land.

His displeasure was even more difficult to hide because of his wife's affection for the children of Holland. Salali would take her daughters, Tayanita and Yona, with her to prepare food and meals for the children of Holland. Onacona, their young brother, would play with the Holland children. Onacona and the Holland children, one boy and one girl, were close in age and enjoyed the toys that Holland would bring them.

Salali knew that her husband's spirit had inner struggles over the friendship that his children had with Holland's children. She continued to pray that he would relent and see that the white man known as Holland and his children were good people, and their color did not brand them as evil.

Dustu continued to provide for his family, and he loved Salali and his children with all the love a man could have. He kept his fear of the white's man influence upon his family in his heart and did not convey it to his wife. However, he could not accompany his wife and children to the white man's house and made little reference to him. Dustu remembered watching his father march to his probable death, by the white man's will. He could not bring himself to see any white man as acceptable to the Great Spirit.

A strange malady swept through the small village as Dustu and Salali's children reached adulthood. The white man called it 'measles,' and it took many lives. The disease infected both Dustu and his daughter, Yona, Yona was able to recover, but Dustu did not.

Salali mourned her husband upon his death and prayed that God would accept him into the heaven promised by the missionaries, even though he had not made an acceptance of the white man's God. Salali felt deep inside that God and the Great Spirit were one, and that God would understand Dustu's life and the heartaches he had endured.

Dustu's children were devastated at their father's death, although they had reached adulthood at that time. Tayanita and Yona had both been spoken for by other Cherokee men in Chief Yonaguska's clan. Onacona had not met a woman he cared to take as his wife and found solace with the grown children of Holland as he wept for his father. Sarah and Josiah were his confidants and friends since they had been small children. Onacona had other friends who were in the Clan, but none as close as Sarah and Josiah.

Holland, Sarah and Josiah's father, was very old and in poor health. Josiah asked Salali to move into their father's house and help with his care. He also felt that Salali should have somewhere to live and be safe now that Dustu had died. Salali moved into the large home and tried to keep Holland as comfortable as possible. He was in much pain and slept much of the time. A bottle of magic sat next to the bed. Salali could not read, but her son said the name of the magic was laudanum. When Holland would wake in pain, the magic would take his pain *away, and he would sleep. Salali tried to feed him whenever he would awake, but he ate little. Salali's prayers included Holland and his journey to the next life. She could tell he would be leaving this life soon.*

Onacona found himself looking upon Sarah with more feelings than friendship. He talked with his mother about his feelings for Sarah. Although Salali knew that Dustu would not approve were he still alive, she felt he knew now that he was in God's kingdom; it would be right. She gave Onacona her blessing because she loved him and wanted his happiness. Salali was sad by the thought of the Cherokee losing their land and possibly in time, their heritage as more and more unions would be made between peoples of different clans. White and red. Salali had a woman friend who had taken a black man for her husband. White and red and black. Were there other clans of other colors in other parts of the world that had not yet made their way to the mountains?

Salali realized that she knew little other than what was in the mountains. Her life had been in the mountains she called home. Perhaps the Great Spirit God had plans that brought all peoples together of all clans. The heaven that she had heard about; would all clans be together singing praises, as the missionaries had said angels did?

Salali lived to old age, enjoying her grandchildren, both Cherokee and mixed clans. She laughed with joy when one of the young ones pointed to her skin and told her that she was brown like the earth. Yes, brown like the earth. Not red, not white, not black. Brown like the earth.

Onacona and Sarah were married by a visiting priest in 1885. Sarah's brother stood with her, as her father was unable to attend. Sarah had six children, one dying in childbirth. While Onacona and Sarah remained on the mountain and made it their home, their children set out to make their home in other parts of this United States. Two of the children married Cherokee and moved closer to the ocean, not far from the mountains. The other three scattered, residing in Tennessee and Florida, and one to Oklahoma, searching for relatives.

ELEVEN

Patch did wake up before Lizzie, and when the coffee was ready, took his cup to the deck and watched the sun climb in the sky. The colors reflected in the trees from the morning sun took his breath away. His prayers required no effort or thought this morning. Who could not praise Him amid such beauty?

Rocking slowly, he pulled the blanket around him closer as he sipped the coffee, feeling the warmth spread through his chest. That he could be sitting here, in the only place he found that could compare to his Sanibel, with Lizzie, the woman he wanted to be with forever. His thankfulness to God didn't seem enough. What could he do to praise God for these blessings? Should this fortune last for even one day, he would be thankful for this day.

A low moan reached his ears. It seemed to come from under the deck. Standing, he looked down and quickly stepped back. Only a few feet down, looking up at him, was a large black bear. The bear had a strange wisp of reddish hair at the top of its head. Silently leaning over to look again, the bear was still looking up at him but making no noise.

"Are you Sheba?" Patch whispered, not sure if the bear heard him. It didn't move, and he didn't know if the bear was a boy or a girl.

The bear cocked its head and backed up, presumably to see him better.

"I love your Lizzie. She's told me about you. She thinks you have some inner spirit that you share with her. She told me that you are her best friend before me. Because she tells you everything. Did she tell you about me, Sheba?"

Patch looked into the bear's eyes, black orbs that seemed to draw him into their depths. Not a sound, no movement. A squeak behind him, and he felt Lizzie's hand on his shoulder. He motioned with a nod of his head to the scene below.

Lizzie looked down at the bear that was staring up at them. "Sheba," she breathed softly. Nodding at the bear, she said, "This is him, this is Patch."

The large bear visibly took a big breath, her back rising. Then, appearing unconcerned, she turned and headed towards the berries left on the vine. Soon there would be none, and Sheba would look elsewhere.

Patch and Lizzie stood watching the bear as she grabbed handful after handful and pushed them into her mouth. Though Sheba never looked their way again, Patch knew she was regarding them with ambivalence.

Lizzie clasped Patch's hand. "She'll come around," she whispered, smiling at her bear.

As if Sheba heard her, she turned and ambled back into the forest.

TWELVE

Patch pulled the Jeep over to the first parking spot on the gravel road. They would need to walk the trail up to Clingman's Dome. Lizzie reached over into the back seat and picked up the small backpack she had placed there. Patch had not asked any questions when she brought it with her. She needed it.

Something extraordinary was going to happen today; Patch knew it.

Lizzie grabbed Patch's hand as they began the climb. "Thank you for helping me with all that stuff in the box. I've been putting it off far too long. It's beginning to make sense. There are blanks, and so many relatives that I never knew about, and don't know if I can find. I feel a deeper kinship with these mountains now. I've always loved the mountains and the cabin, but knowing that your ancestors walked these grounds two hundred years ago..."

Patch looked down at the smiling face of his love. "I get it. That's the feeling I get when I'm on the beach. We know that members of our family were close by to the same spot, and loved and cried and died. That kind of knowledge makes love so powerful. Can we love someone that we never knew? I feel love for Magdalena, my great-something grandmother."

Lizzie nodded. "Yes, like I feel love and a connection with Dustu and Salali. They could not know what came after, but do you think that maybe they thought about it? You know that Magdalena thought about her grandchildren, about who came after. She talked about her grandchildren reading her journal someday. Can we love those who come after? The ones we know nothing about, whether they are good and loving people?"

"I think we can pray for those that come after. There's something else about this feeling of sharing the space of the mountain or the ocean. What about in Jerusalem? In Bethlehem, in Nazareth. We must go there one day, Lizzie!" Patch's voice lowered, serious and thoughtful.

"Yes, I want to go there, too. To walk where He walked, to see the land where He lived as a man. Jesus. Our Lord. Yes, you're right. We must go to the Holy Land. That connection is for all men and women!" Lizzie squeezed Patch's hand, then let go.

"Okay! Enough serious talk. Let's pick it up. We've got a mountain to climb!" Lizzie laughed as she started taking giant steps up the paved path. You could easily make the half-mile hike in under an hour, but Patch wanted to stop at every bench they reached the last time they did this. It was a steep incline, but well worth the view at the top.

Patch followed, laughing and complaining. "I'm stopping at the first bench!" he yelled. He watched her go ahead of him. There were few people on the path this early; it would be easy to follow her. He had decided long ago that he would follow her anywhere. Lizzie had convinced him to join her on another trip a few years back, in 1969. The road trip that started their journey of being together. He thought of that trip as the beginning.

THIRTEEN
1969

Patch pulled the little Jeep in front of Lizzie's dorm. He hadn't been excited about this trip she wanted to take, but he had heard a lot about it from some of his friends. All these great bands giving a free concert – what's not to like? Lizzie had the map, and they were off to a farm in Bethel, New York. If they headed north and reached Woodstock, they had gone too far. That's about as much as he knew. Classes wouldn't start for another couple of weeks, so they had returned to campus early to leave together on this 'great adventure' as Lizzie called it.

A few minutes later, they were headed down the interstate, first to Knoxville, then north. Lizzie was talking non-stop about her Biology class and the professor that never changed his voice from a monotone. Patch thought she was probably as nervous as he was, and that was why she was talking so much. They had never been away together. Not alone. He didn't know how this trip was going to work out. But he did know that he did not want to lose what they had together. Before they stopped for the night, there must be a heart-to-heart talk. Nothing held back.

"You haven't heard a word I said!" Lizzie flicked her fingers on his arm.

Reaching over to her, he laid his hand on her shoulder. "Sure I have, but I do have to pay attention to the road."

"Okay, so what did I just ask you?" Lizzie asked.

"Something about the lab work the Prof' gave you?" Patch thought he had heard something like that.

"No, no, no. I've got the lab work. Now I have to write a paper with my conclusions. I don't have any conclusions!" Lizzie sighed. "Never mind. I don't want to think about this now. We have a fantastic weekend ahead of us! You're excited, too, right?"

"Sure, I am." Patch glanced over at Lizzie. She was staring at the road, the windows down, her dark hair blowing with the wind. "Let's pull over before it gets too dark. If I'm going to pitch a tent, I need daylight to do it."

"Oh yeah. I brought sandwiches and chips. Maybe we can get on the other side of Knoxville before we stop. I think there's a campground close to the state line." Lizzie pulled out an 8-track. "Here, I've got the new 'Credence Clearwater' tape. Let's try it out. They are supposed to be there, you know."

Hours and more than one 8-track later, they stopped at a small campground a mile off the interstate. Taking the tents and sleeping bags out of the Jeep, Patch set up the small pup tents in just a few minutes. Joining Lizzie on a blanket, the sun sitting low in the sky barely visible through the trees, he picked up a sandwich and ate.

"Here's a Coke. They're not really cold, the ice melted, but it's better than nothing." Lizzie handed the can over, and Patch's hand covered hers.

Taking the can and placing it next to him on the ground, Patch turned back to Lizzie. "Let's talk about something."

Lizzie grinned. "Something? Okay, what about this amazing concert we're going to see? We can camp out there; we can see all these other people. You know, somebody said that there might be a couple of hundred people there. Won't that be something!"

"That's not exactly what I was talking about." Patch took her hands in his. "We haven't talked about this before. We're here together, you know, by ourselves. And we've never, well, we never..."

"Yeah, and we're not going to tonight, either! Really, Patch? I'm not ready for that." Lizzie was uncomfortable; Patch would tell.

"No, Lizzie, you've got me wrong. I'm not asking; truly, I'm not. We just haven't talked about it. I'm glad you're not, that you don't, well, you know." Patch stopped. He knew that he wasn't making sense.

Taking a deep breath, he reached for one of Lizzie's hands, holding it between both of his. "Lizzie, look at me."

Lizzie looked into his eyes and saw nothing but concern for her there. This man was a kind person; he would not hurt her. And she didn't want to hurt him.

Patch continued, "I am so proud that you are who you are. I know I've never said it, but I'm falling in love with you, falling hard. I don't want anything to mess that up. I'll wait for you, for us, for as long as you want. If it's to be, it will be, right?"

"I can't talk about this now, not now. I'm not who you think I am. I know that's not the way things are now in the world, but I can't. You don't understand." Lizzie pulled her hand away from his. She knew that she wasn't making a lot of sense.

"But Lizzie! That's a good thing! I believe as you do. I can't say that I've always been the good guy, but I want to be the good guy for you. And I will be. I will never pressure you. Kissing you brings me happiness like you couldn't believe!"

Patch reached over to put his arm around her shoulder, but Lizzie stood and crossed her arms.

"There are things you don't know about me, Patch. Things that I wish..." Lizzie shook her head. "I don't want to talk about this now. Let's get some sleep. We need to make an early start tomorrow morning, right?" She turned to him and smiled.

Patch could see through the smile. He had known her long enough to see the contour of her face by memory, and the lines between her eyes gave her away. She was sad or worried, maybe upset. Something was amiss, but he let it go. It could wait.

"Sure, yeah. I'm tired, and we need to make it a long day tomorrow to make it as far as we can." Patch picked up the trash and walked it over to the metal can hanging on a short pole. "Do I need to tell you a bedtime story? Or maybe sing a lullaby?"

Lizzie laughed. "Only if you want to wake up with bugs in your sleeping bag!"

FOURTEEN

Rolling thunder woke them the next morning. Quickly taking down the small tents and throwing everything in the Jeep, Patch and Lizzie felt the first few drops of rain begin to fall as they raised the top over the windshield.

"I hope we're not riding in this all day," Lizzie said as she shivered with the cold rain in her hair.

"Yeah, outside concerts with rain is not a great draw for a crowd, either," Patch replied, as he drove toward the interstate. "Let's grab some coffee and maybe a banana somewhere before we get too far. Maybe the rain will pass us by while we stop. I need to fill up with gas," he said as the rain began falling in sheets against the canvas top.

Two hours later, the rain was still falling. The coffee and bananas were gone, and Patch had found a leak in the old canvas top. Lizzie laughed and placed a bottle next to it, but the movement displaced any drops of water from landing in the bottle.

"I hope this isn't going to follow us all the way," Patch said, his hands gripping the steering wheel. Water was pooling on the freeway, and he had watched two cars in front of him slide into oncoming traffic before correcting themselves. The road itself wasn't in pristine shape, holes and uneven pavement stretching for miles.

It seemed the rain was beginning to let up when Patch felt, rather than heard, the pop of the right front tire. "Oh no," Patch said as he made his way to the side of the road, pulling out of traffic and into the flat grassy area.

Lizzie grabbed the seat. "What happened?"

"I think we blew a tire," Patch said as he turned off the ignition. He looked over at her and smiled. "It's okay. I'll change the flat, and we'll be on our way."

"You're going to be soaking wet! Just wait until the rain lets up some." Lizzie shook her head, looking through the windshield at the sky.

"A few minutes, maybe. I'm not sure it's going to get much better." Patch peered up into the sky from his side window. "It looks pretty gloomy. I don't see any blue sky anywhere right now."

Shaking his head, Patch opened the door to step out, then pulled the door shut again. Banging his fist against the steering wheel, he groaned.

"What?" Lizzie looked at him, bewildered.

"The tire. The spare. It's flat. I changed a flat a couple of months ago, and I never fixed it. I don't have a spare. The spare has a hole the size of a quarter in it." Patch looked over at her. She was looking at him, eyes widening.

"What are we going to do?" she asked. "I guess we can walk to a station, right?"

"Yeah, but you don't have to come. Stay here with the Jeep. I'll take off the tire and roll it with me. Maybe this one isn't too bad, and they can patch it."

"No. I don't want to be here by myself! I'll walk with you." Lizzie opened the car door.

"Please, Liz, stay in the car. I really want you to stay with the Jeep. Lock it up, and don't open the door for anyone. You can roll down the window a bit if anyone stops. There's plenty of traffic on the road; I don't think anybody will bother you. I hate to leave you here, but it's a mess out here, and this is the best thing. Okay?" Patch looked at her, pleading.

Lizzie didn't say anything; she only nodded.

Patch got out and left a few minutes later, rolling the damaged tire up the road. It was still raining, but he could see in front of him. Dripping with water, he was surprised when a truck pulled over and rolled down the window.

"Hey there, son. Need a ride to the station up thereabouts?" A man peered out from under an old baseball cap. "I'll be glad to give you a lift. That your Jeep back there?"

Patch turned and looked back toward the Jeep. He could barely make it out through the rain but doubted that Lizzie could see him. "Sir, that would be great. I appreciate it. I'll ride in the back; I'm soaking."

"Nonsense. Throw the tire in, hop in up here. This old truck has seen a lot worse than a little rain thrown in." The man moved an old jacket from the passenger side and threw it in the little space behind the seat. "I see a fellow in a bad way on the side of the road; I'm going to stop and try to help. You'd do the same, wouldn't ya?"

"I hope I would, yes, sir. My daddy says he hopes that the day never comes that we can't stop and help someone, but I wonder sometimes. You know, there are lots of bad people out there." Patch raised his hands in the air. "I'm not one of them!"

Laughing, the man nodded. "Didn't think you were. But I reckon you're right. Ya know, that Tate girl out in California, that was just awful. I hope they catch those murderers. Just a few days ago, you heard about that?"

"Yes, it was awful. And somebody else the next day. They think it's the same people, a bunch of them." Patch looked over at the man, deciding that he could trust him. "My name is Patch; actually, it's Patrick Delamar, but everyone calls me Patch."

"Nice to meet you, Patch, the name's Herb Patterson. Just on my way home to the boss. My wife, that is. Rosie. She's got me some good cooking on; I'll betcha. But she would be mighty upset with me if I drove on by a needy fellow on the side of the road. She'd skin me alive; she would."

"Thank you, Mr. Patterson. You're a life-saver, yes, sir. My friend and I were on our way to this big concert, and I had this flat and no spare to speak of..." Patch shook his head, ashamed that he had not prepared better for the trip.

"Your friend, you got somebody back in that Jeep, son?" Herb Patterson glanced over at Patch.

"Yes, sir, my girlfriend, Lizzie. She's waiting for me to get back. All locked up; she won't open the door to anybody." Patch didn't sound convinced, even to himself.

"I got an idea that maybe we oughta do something about that. We're almost there now. I'll take the tire and wait on getting it fixed. You take my truck on back there to your girl. I'll get Tom up there at the station to bring me and the tire to you when it's finished. I don't like your girl being back there by herself, nope, none at all." Herb Patterson shook his head.

"Sir, that's awful nice of you. I don't know how I could repay you; this is just so over what I could ever expect from a good Samaritan like you." Patch was astounded at the man's trust.

Patch's rescuer took the tire from the back of the truck and waved Patch's money away with his hand. "I'll take care of this tire; you go on back there to your girl. I'll be along shortly."

Although no one had stopped, Lizzie had been frightened that someone would stop and concerned that she would not know whether to unlock the door. As a strange truck began slowing near her, she held her breath. When she realized it was Patch driving, she was confused but smiled at him. Lizzie was also surprised when Patch told her about his new friend, Herb.

Only a few minutes had passed when Herb Patterson returned with the repaired tire. The rain had taken a break, although thunder was becoming louder with the promise of more storms to come.

"Let's get this tire back on, boy. Oh, I'm sorry, Patch, isn't it? You and your girl can come on back to my house for some dinner. Nope, won't take no for an answer. You can explain to my Rosie why I'm so late, there you go." Herb Patterson was placing the tire back when Patch handed him the wrench.

Looking up at Lizzie as he squatted beside the man putting his tire back on, he shrugged his shoulders. She just grinned back at him.

FIFTEEN

Following Patterson's truck to his home that he assured them was only a few miles away, Patch and Lizzie decided they would ask their new friend if he knew of a campground nearby. Although it was still early in the day, barely 2:00 pm, after they ate with the Patterson's, neither of them wanted to continue to drive in the rain.

Plans should never be written in stone, Patch had thought. God has a way of letting you know that your plan is not His plan.

They had eaten a hearty dinner prepared by Herb's wife, Rosie, who insisted they stay the night when they asked about a campground. There were two bedrooms across from each other, and she promised them a hot breakfast before they started on their way.

A comical and friendly game of Scrabble followed dinner, and then a lazy afternoon listening to the Pattersons brag on their grandchildren and share their love of Jesus. Both of the Pattersons were active in their church and taught Sunday School classes to the younger children in the community. Herb drove a small church bus he had refitted from a junkyard so that he could pick up the children in the surrounding mountain community that didn't get a chance to go to church.

A light supper of grilled cheese and tomato soup completed the day as the clouds rolled away to broadcast a spectacular sunset, complete with a vanishing rainbow.

A beautiful starry night greeted them despite the storm that had finally made its way northward. Leaving Herb and Rosie to watch their favorite television show, 'Bonanza,' Patch and Lizzie made their way to an old swing in the Patterson's back yard that overlooked a meadow dotted with sheep, baby lambs following the ewes around.

Light from an almost full moon bathed the wet grass with sprinkles of glitter. Patch looked over at Lizzie and put his arm around her shoulder as he saw her shudder.

"Cold?" he asked, concerned. It was August, after all, and quite warm even though it had been raining and the sun was gone.

"No, not cold. Scared." Lizzie sat, back straight against the swing. "I have to talk to you; I have to tell you stuff. Stuff that you won't like, stuff that will make you want to take me back home and run as far away as you can."

Patch's slight hesitation before saying anything made Lizzie bite her lip. He would run, she was sure he would.

"Lizzie? Whatever you have to say to me, just say it. I thought we were getting along pretty good, that we were moving this thing we have; that we were moving it somewhere." He looked at her and could see the tears waiting to fall down her cheeks. "What have I done? I haven't made you think that I wanted something that I was trying to, you know, do something to you. Oh come on, Lizzie, what is this about?"

"No, nothing like that. It's not anything you've done, Patch, it's me. You're not going to like what I have to tell you." Lizzie couldn't look at him; she kept staring in front of her.

"Oh. I see. It's someone else, isn't it?" Patch sighed. He guessed he should have known. Someone as great as Lizzie wouldn't settle for him. "But why would you want to go on this trip with me? To let me down easy?"

"Patch, hush, just hush. No, you doofus, you're the only one." Lizzie smiled through her tears, then put her head down in her hands. "You're the one that's not going to want me anymore."

Patch reached over and turned Lizzie's face to his with his finger. "You have won my heart, don't you know that? I know you, Lizzie. I know your heart for Jesus, I know the love in you. There is nothing, I tell you, nothing that could change what I feel for you." Talking about the Bible together had sealed Patch's feelings. He sensed that God had put them together; he believed in God's plan for them. To hear that Lizzie felt the same way, that there was no one else, calmed his fear. He wanted to talk about their future together. Whatever secret she wanted to share with him, how bad could it be? Of course, they had both made mistakes, who had not? But really, how bad could it be? Patch believed in God's power, in His plan for all of his children, marred though they were. He hoped it was not wishful thinking on his part that God had a plan for him and Lizzie together.

"Patch, stop," said Lizzie, sensing that he was going to say something else. "This is going to be hard enough, and I'm going to cry through it because there's no other way, but I've got to tell you. I could just break it off and save you the trouble, but I owe it to you to tell you the truth. You're right, we've fallen in love, haven't we?"

Lizzie sounded wistful to Patch, sad even. What could she possibly have to say to him, he thought.

"Let me tell you everything from the start," Lizzie said. "It will take a while, but I need you not to say anything, please. Just hear it all. I trust you, Patch, with my deepest pain. You are the only one..."

"Okay, Lizzie, okay. I'll be quiet. Just tell me, don't judge me on how I will feel about it." Patch looked into her eyes and nodded.

SIXTEEN

The story unfolded. Lizzie began, speaking softly. Patch had to lean in to hear her. As she continued, he rested his head in his hands.

"I dated who I thought was my 'one and only' in high school. We had been going 'steady' for two years. He was a year older than me; he respected me and didn't pressure me to do anything. He told me that holding my hand and kissing me was enough because he knew that we would be perfect for each other when we married. We talked about it; we talked about it a lot. He was going to college, and I was going to join him when I graduated high school. Everything was perfect. I thought it was, anyway. I was naïve; I see that now. My dreams with him being a doctor, and I would be working in the hospital as a nurse or something, just silly, girlish dreams. The day before he was to leave for college, he told me he thought we should date other people, you know, just to be sure. I knew it was over. He was leaving for college, and I wouldn't see him again. I was right, you know. He never called, and when I saw a friend of his at church, he told me that my 'one and only' was involved with someone else, and it was serious. He was going to transfer to where she was going to school in another state. It was kind of clear this was not a new development. I had been a fool." Lizzie took a deep breath and stretched her back.

Patch didn't say anything. Lizzie wasn't looking at him, but he was sure she had not finished her story. She continued, her voice sounding louder, almost as if she had pulled on a strength deep inside.

"I called a friend, well, kind of a friend. Marcia wasn't close or anything, but we had talked in science class. She had asked me to join her with a group when they went to town for a party. I told her I had broken up with my boyfriend, and I needed to go out and have a good time. She was all for it. I told my parents I was spending the night with a friend at church and met Marcia at her house. We went to this nightclub just outside of town. They weren't real particular about looking at ID's, and they served us drinks as soon as we walked in. I didn't even know what to order, but Marcia did. She ordered for both of us, and she kept on ordering. I remember thinking that it was pretty good stuff, especially the second or third drink. We met some guys there, I don't know if Marcia knew them or not, but we danced. We danced a lot. And I drank a lot." Lizzie turned and looked at Patch, determination written across her face.

"I want you to know that this was my fault, nobody else's. I don't blame Marcia or the guy. I was the one that decided to go to this nightclub with Marcia. I could have said no. I was drinking.

I could have said no. I didn't say no. And what happened afterward, well, I could have said no earlier and I would be able to remember what happened."

Lizzie closed her eyes. Patch wanted to say something, to reach out to her, but something held him back. He wanted her to finish, to tell him everything. He had to know.

Not opening her eyes, she laid her head against the back of the swing. "I woke up the next morning in bed with the guy I had been dancing with. I didn't have any clothes on. It was pretty clear what had happened. I was so ashamed. And mad at myself. Here I had held myself back from a boy I thought I loved, and then a one-night guy that I never wanted to see again."

Patch could see Lizzie take a shuddering breath, trying to hold in tears. He reached for her hand, but she pushed it away.

"No, I'm not finished." She looked over at Patch with tears running down her face. "If I only had to tell you that I'm not the virgin I wish I could be for you, I could ask for your forgiveness. Even then, you deserve better. But that's not all."

Patch couldn't hold himself back. "Lizzie, I love you. I wish we were both pure for each other, but that can't stop us from being the couple that I believe God wants us to be! We all make mistakes. The guy, he took advantage..."

Lizzie broke in, "No, we're not going to talk about him. I've never seen him again, and I don't intend to. Names are not important; I only told you Marcia's because well, she moved to another state with her family." Lizzie turned again to Patch and said, "Don't you see, Patch, this was all my doing. I made the mistakes. I was ashamed and promised myself that I would never do that again. I prayed and prayed. I asked God to forgive me. I had another year of high school! I felt like I had ruined my life, but I moved forward. I trusted that God would forgive me; He would show me the way."

The tears fell in earnest now. Patch didn't dare interrupt.

"Three months later, I knew that I was pregnant." She gave a little snort, almost a mocking laugh. "Don't let anyone say that only one time can't get you pregnant. It can."

Patch's breath caught. A baby. But where was the child? His emotions were in freefall. The knot in his stomach twisted.

Lizzie looked straight ahead, tears streaming down her face. Her eyes were not blinking, seeming to look back into a dark cave.

"I had no choice. I had to go to my parents. At the time, I thought it was the hardest thing I would ever have to do – disappoint my mom and dad, who had done everything to make sure I had everything I needed, who loved me more than themselves, these parents that I loved so much, I was going to hurt them."

Lizzie stood and looked up into the starlit sky. Patch had to listen carefully to hear her; her voice was soft.

"Mom cried, and then cried some more. I don't remember a lot of what she said; she told me later that she didn't mean it. Daddy hugged me and asked me who it belonged to. I'm not sure what he was planning on doing, but I just told him that the boy was not in the picture. Then he asked me what I wanted to do; did I want to keep it?" Lizzie sobbed, and when Patch stood to comfort her, she held her arm out, shaking her head. He sat back down, waiting for her to continue. Patch wasn't sure that he wanted to hear the rest.

"Somebody, I think it was mom, said that we would go to the doctor the next day and figure it out." Lizzie took a ragged breath. "We went to a doctor referred by a counselor at church. I won't go through all the gory details, but the doctor said that he didn't think the pregnancy would pan out, there was some problem or the other, and I should consider eliminating the pregnancy. That's how he put it – eliminating the pregnancy."

"An abortion." Patch said the words before he thought about it. He heard the catch in Lizzie's breath and couldn't look at her.

"I went along with whatever plans were made. My parents and I flew to New York, and when we came back, I wasn't pregnant anymore. We cried, but we didn't talk about it. Daddy asked me if this is what I wanted, and I just nodded. Mom made the arrangements and said this was best for everyone. I didn't want to think about it. I didn't want to think about anything. I wanted to die."

Lizzie laughed again, that horrible derisive laugh Patch had heard earlier.

She choked out, "I remember the night that I realized I was pregnant and had to tell my parents. I prayed. Patch, I prayed that God would give me a terrible disease. Anything besides that I was pregnant. I couldn't hurt my parents if I was dying, could I? So silly. So bad."

Lizzie sat down again on the swing, holding her head high as if to say she was going to finish this, no matter the consequences.

"The doctor in New York said that he could not find a heartbeat, and I held on to that for a long time. But I'm not that dumb. How many young girls did he tell that? A lot, I bet. It was a horrible place. Dark, with all these girls and women lying in beds in one long room. Crying. All of them. Crying. Sometimes screaming. When I remember that room, I only think one thing. Hell. There was nothing good there, Patch. Not me, not anyone. But I felt sorry for the other girls there. There was this one woman right next to me. She held my hand for a time, telling me it would only hurt for a little while. She said she didn't want to be there, but she couldn't have any more babies. She had too many already. I looked at her and wondered why she got pregnant, but then I remembered that I didn't want to be pregnant, either. I sometimes wonder how the other women in that room feel now. Once it's really clear what you've done. The mistake was not getting pregnant – that was a choice." When Patch started to speak, Lizzie shook her head.

"Oh, I know. I know that there are some women out there that didn't have a choice. They were forced and raped, but most made a choice to have sex and not be prepared. But the baby never had a choice. The mistake, the sin, the evil...that was the abortion."

Lizzie laid her hand on Patch's knee until he raised his eyes to hers. "I have a baby in heaven. A baby that never had a chance. Can my child even forgive me? I don't see how. That I took the life of that child, that I am the monster that did that. I live with that every day. And I think about him or her every day. Sometimes it's a little boy riding a horsey stick around in the clouds, or sometimes it's a little girl in a swing. Every year on the day I ended the life of that precious child, I grieve. I pray for forgiveness, and I ask Jesus to watch over that little life. I beg for a chance to be with my baby someday." That laugh again. "Oh, I know how that sounds. It doesn't matter. I know what I did. I took a life."

Patch couldn't speak. He didn't know what to say. Lizzie seemed to be talking to herself more than to him. She didn't stop.

"It would be simple to think that abortion was okay, that there wasn't life there until birth or whenever someone says it is. I can't see how any woman that looks down deep in her soul could feel that way. A life. A life. Regardless of how it starts, you are given this perfect gift of growing a baby in your body. That's a huge responsibility but an even more abundant blessing. That's God's child in there. From the moment of conception, that is God's child. What does the scripture say? It's in Jeremiah; I read it often to remind me what I have done. 'Before I had formed you in the womb, I knew you.' Abortion is an evil that seems to try to find a foothold in our world. I let it drag me in, and I became the evil that it brought. My choice had consequences. The consequences should have been mine, not my child's. I killed my unborn child. I live with that every day." A long sigh. She looked down and closed her eyes. Her story was finished.

Patch was unsure of what to say. Shook to his core, he didn't know what the feelings in his heart were telling him. He knew that he needed to say something.

"Patch?"

He couldn't look up at her, not until he knew what to say.

"It's okay, Patch. As I said, I live with this every day. I will live with it until I die and after.

I pray that I can be forgiven. But I don't know if I can. You do not have to live with this. That's why we can't work. I can't give you what you deserve—a good person. I'm not that. I don't deserve what you can give a wife. I don't deserve any of that." Lizzie stood and walked toward the house. "I'm going in and going to bed. I'm exhausted." She hesitated and then said, "I'm sorry, Patch. I shouldn't have let it get this far. You are so good; you don't deserve this."

Lizzie had gone inside and shut the door when Patch fell to the ground, sounds of grief bursting forth. Lizzie had thrown his world in a tailspin. What should he do? What could he do? Did this change how he felt? He had only one answer. He had to pray. He had to pray a lot. On his knees, he asked for God to guide him.

SEVENTEEN

Patch came down the steps to the bright kitchen. Mrs. Patterson had indeed made breakfast, complete with gravy, grits, and all the homemade biscuits anyone could eat. As he started to sit down, Rosie Patterson touched his arm. "Why don't you go and get your girl? She's outside in the swing." The look in her eyes told him she knew that Lizzie was hurting. All he could do was nod.

"Lizzie?" He spoke softly. She turned to him, her eyes red. She hadn't slept much, which was easy to see. As she started to talk, he touched his finger to her lips. "No, let me."

Patch sat down on the swing beside her, silently praying that God would guide him in his next words. Lizzie was looking down at her hands, and he didn't touch her. He looked off in the distance at the sky as it became bright with the sun beating down on the glistening dew.

"Lizzie, I love you. I've told you that before, and it remains. We, us, we've only just started. I would not be here with you unless God had led me to you; I truly believe that. We have hearts that blend into each other, that will learn to beat as one, as God intended. That is our future. I believe it."

"Patch..." Lizzie began, shaking her head.

"No, wait, I'm not finished." Patch held up his hand to silence her but didn't look her way, not yet. He couldn't look at her until he could touch her. And he couldn't touch her until he felt she understood.

"You have borne a burden on your soul. I understand that, although I can never bear that burden for you. But I can help you carry it. I will talk with you, hold you, pray with you, cry with you. I will do all of this and help you carry this burden until you find the faith to give it up and let God take it. Accept His love and forgiveness."

Patch heard Lizzie take a deep breath. He turned to her. "Lizzie?" She raised her eyes to his.

"Lizzie, forgive yourself and accept His amazing grace. You and I will pray for your child in heaven. We will both love your child in heaven, now and when heaven is our home, too."

Lizzie reached for him, and he took her in his arms. Holding her tightly, he whispered in her ear, "Dear Lizzie, don't give up on me. On us. We just started."

Lizzie nodded in his shoulder. "Okay," she said softly.

EIGHTEEN
1975

Lizzie slowed to allow him to catch up. "Need a break?" she asked, pointing to a bench that was off the path a few feet ahead.

"That would be wonderful," Patch exclaimed, always amazed at Lizzie's ability to continue uphill without breathing any differently.

Sitting on the carved bench, reaching down to feel the smooth wood beneath her fingers, Lizzie sighed. "This reminds me of the bench that Maddie sat on outside her cabin. We have a background of interesting ancestors, don't we?"

"Yes, I guess we do. Between Maddie and Gaspar, and Dustu and Salali, we managed to bring the oceans to the mountains, haven't we?" Patch reached over and clasped Lizzie's hand in his.

"I wish...I wish I could be different. As good as they were. As good as you are."

"Lizzie, don't say that. I've had my share of sins. Vietnam will never leave me. There will be a place deep inside, forever reminding me that I returned alive, but wounded in my soul. A choice between your life and someone else's is much too easy to make in a single moment in time but lives with you forever. The face you saw at that moment haunts your nightmares."

"I'm sorry, Patch. I know we haven't talked much about your time there. You change the subject each time I bring it up..."

Patch nodded. "It's not easy to talk about. But that's for another time. We have a lifetime to tell our stories, to help each other find the other side and stay there." He smiled at her, taking a wayward strand of her hair and placing it behind her ear.

"You are so good. You are a good person, Lizzie; you are good for me. Sometimes I doubt myself; I know how you feel. I search for my faith; I keep assuring myself that it is still there, I just have to wait for it to kick in, you know? My mom had a scare about breast cancer, and I was terrified. It didn't matter how much I knew that God was there. I knew it in my heart, you know, but I couldn't convince my head. My thoughts, my doubts. It was more terrifying than the nights I felt so alone in 'Nam. You know, sometimes, we don't know why things happen. Things don't always turn out perfect, or the way we want them to. But we have to hang onto faith. Knowing that God loves us and will take care of us. I know that we lose that faith sometimes, or we forget it. Then we remind ourselves of what a great God we have. Think about your mom or dad – what would they not do for you? Our God, our Father in heaven – He is perfect – He will never leave you or forsake you, no matter what, like your parents, but even more. Lizzie, He was with you in your darkest hour, when you needed Him the most, even though you didn't know He was there. And He is there now and always. Because He loves you. He grieves with you and wants you to accept His love, His forgiveness. I don't know how else to tell you, Lizzie. I feel like I'm preaching to you, and that's not what I want."

"No, no, you're not." Lizzie looked in his eyes and saw that tears were streaming down his face as they were hers. "That certainty you have. I want that; I want that so much. But my baby, my baby that I..."

He knew that she would deal with this pain for a long time to come. But he had faith that each time God would pick her back up. He wanted to be there to help do that, too. Patch took her hands in his. "Stop. Close your eyes, Lizzie. Your baby, picture that baby right now. You told me you've done that before, seen your child in your dreams. I want you to see Jesus holding that baby, smiling into that baby's eyes, and that baby, your baby, Lizzie, is laughing. Laughing, because how could anyone, baby or adult, not be happy to be in His arms? Look, Lizzie."

Lizzie had her eyes closed, almost squinting. Tears sprang again from under her lashes. "Yes, I see." A deep breath, taking it in, letting it out slowly. "I see." She smiled, a brilliant, beautiful smile, though her eyes remain closed.

Patch stepped back, still holding onto her hands. It seemed as if a light was shining around her. A very pale but clear light. He shook his head, trying to focus his eyes. Maybe it was because she was seeing...what?

Then all he could see were her eyes, looking into his. Nodding her head with tears streaming down her face, she seemed unable to speak. But he knew.

Lizzie reached for the small backpack she had placed on the ground. Inside was a small box with a ribbon wrapped around it. Untying the ribbon, Lizzie took out an old faded plane ticket from New York, stamped and used.

"This is what I have. Physically, this is all I have. It reminds me each day of my sin. The man that handed me this ticket had no idea he was giving me my sin on a piece of paper. I don't want to look at this anymore. I always want to remember my child and forever beg forgiveness. But I can't look at my sin anymore. God doesn't want me to, does He?" She looked up at Patch.

"No, He doesn't. God wants you to know that He forgives you because you asked. Because you believe. You don't need a piece of paper to remind you of your child in heaven, Lizzie. We'll pray every day for our child in heaven. Ours, Lizzie. Your child is my child."

Smiling through her tears, she said, "Let's go to the top, then, and I'll let this go into the deep mountains, my sin washed away as the mountains meet the ocean."

The last steps up the mountain didn't seem quite as steep to Patch, and Lizzie held his hand, matching her stride to his. As they looked over the rail at the top of the Dome, Lizzie held out her hand, and the small piece of paper sailed down the side of the mountain, the wind catching it and blowing it as it would a feather.

Turning to him, she reached over to his jacket pocket and pulled out the small box inside.

Opening it, she looked up at him. He had waited for this woman in his life. He had prayed for her, and God had placed her in his life. He had prayed that she would find the faith she needed. In God and in him. To be his wife. He took the ring out and placed it, once again, on her finger.

She smiled. "I love you. Yes. Yes. YES!"

Though they were not alone at the top of the Dome, Patch took her in his arms and kissed her, long and tenderly. Hearing the animated voices around them, they separated and looked around. Everyone was pointing down straight down.

Looking over the rail, Patch and Lizzie saw a bear reared on its hind legs scratching its back against a tall cedar. It almost seemed as if Sheba was smiling.

NINETEEN
1976

The small church nestled in the valley would only hold a few people. Patch stood inside, waiting to take his place at the altar with the pastor of Lizzie's home church in Knoxville. He and Lizzie had seen this little church on their way back from the cabin several months ago, on the day that the love of his life had said yes. Something about the way it nestled with the mountains rising on each side spoke to both of them. A small creek ran beside the little white chapel, and you could hear the waters rushing over the rocks from inside. Although the ocean was several hundred miles away, this small community seemed to tell of seas and mountains joining together.

Patch smiled to himself. At least, that's what Lizzie said. And he would marry her wherever she chose. He looked around at the visitors seated in the old wooden pews—family and close friends for both of them. Neither of them wanted a big wedding, choosing to save their money for a trip planned next year to the Holy Land.

Lizzie was staring in the mirror in the small room off the vestibule when Patch's mother, Sheila Delamar, walked in. Beth Oliver had just left the room to check on Lizzie's father. He was nervously waiting to walk his daughter down the aisle.

"You are beautiful," Sheila said softly. "This dress, so soft and flowing, blue like the sky. It's perfect." Lizzie's future mother-in-law ran the light blue cloth over her hand with understanding. "The color of Magdalena's dress? I'm sure she's very pleased."

Looking over at the flowers wrapped in blue and yellow ribbons, Sheila nodded. "Those are beautiful flowers. What are they?"

Lizzie picked up the small bouquet. "They're trout lilies. They grow wild in the mountains. The Cherokee believed that when it was blooming, the fishing would be plentiful, and there would be a great feast." She smiled as she thought of Dustu and Salali.

Lizzie turned and placed her hand in Sheila's. "Thank you," she said with a smile on her face.

Sheila Delamar looked at the young woman who had won the heart of her son. "For?"

"Patch. I love him so very much. And I don't deserve him. But I promise to love him forever and try my very best to make him happy." Lizzie spoke softly as she clasped both hands around Sheila's.

"I have something for you," Sheila said as she took her hand away and reached into her purse. "Something old," she said as she pulled out a tattered, ancient Bible tied together with ribbons of blue.

Lizzie looked at the old Bible, and her breath caught. "Oh!"

"Yes, it's Maddie's, given to her by her mother. It's not in good shape, the reason for the ribbon. The ribbons have been replaced many times over. When I received it from Nolan's mother, they were also blue. I've continued the tradition, I guess. We used this Bible at our marriage; the minister held it as we took our vows. I thought you might want the same? No pressure, though, I promise. It is yours now; I only hope the old faded pages will hold together for another 100 years." Sheila put the Bible in Lizzie's hands. "I better go, Nolan is wondering what is taking me so long, I'm sure."

Lizzie looked down at the old Bible and remembered the many times Maddie had written about it in her journal. Carefully untying the ribbons, she opened to the first page. The script was barely visible, but a few words were clear. Part of the name Magdalena was written in an elaborate flourish. Lizzie ran her hand over the print. A woman two hundred years ago had written this and given it to her daughter. A daughter she never saw again, as far as Lizzie knew. How very sad.

Lizzie carefully closed the Bible and held it reverently. Maddie and Gaspar had poured over the words in this Bible for understanding and faith. She closed her eyes and offered a prayer of thanksgiving for the faith that carried over through generations for both she and Patch.

As Lizzie tried to tie the ribbons, the old book wouldn't close together as it had before. As she checked the cover, a small piece of paper dropped to the floor from an old rip in the inside binding.

Lizzie picked it up and could easily read the name on the outside of the folded sheet, faded though it was. 'Magdalena' it read. As she opened the paper and began reading the old script, she remembered the note that Maddie had placed in the Bible. The letter that Gaspar had left her. The love letter.

*My Magdalena, my Maddie girl; That God above would allow me to kiss you, even that He would allow you to have feelings for me, speaks of His unfailing forgiveness should we beg Him of it. And I do beg Him to forgive me of my transgressions, but not of my feelings of desire for you. As Solomon proclaims in the named book of the Bible: '**I have found the one whom my soul loves**.' And it is you. It is you whom I love, whom I desire, whom I want to hold close to my body and explore the passions between us. I want to know your laughter as my own voice, your wisdom and patience as my innermost thoughts. I want to absorb all of these things into my being, as we complete each other. Until we meet again, I ask you to consider me. I will ask for your hand. For your forever hand, in this world and the next. His Will be done.*

Yours,

Jose Gaspar

AFTERWORD

We are all a product of what has come before. Our linkage to the past. How we see the world, how we react to trials, how we love, how we hate. Patch and Lizzie are so much more than what we see. They are both products of extraordinary ancestry, through the fictional story told. The islands of Sanibel and Captiva are ripe for wondrous stories, with adventure, mystery, and of course, romance.

Though the pirate Gaspar is a popular figure in Florida folklore, there is no evidence that he actually existed. According to legend, Captiva got its name from pirate captain José Gaspar (Gasparilla), holding his female prisoners on the island for ransom (or worse). However, the supposed existence of José Gaspar is sourced from an advertising brochure of an early 20th-century developer and may be wholly fabricated.

I first heard the story of Jose Gaspar while on a boat ride around the islands. The story intrigued me, as pirates stories do. But what if the pirate turned out to be a good guy? Especially if he is the handsome, swashbuckling type! I also latched onto the story of ransomed women. There had to be at least one woman who would stand up to him, right?

Magdalena was that woman. Gaspar was that pirate. And the story began. I had such fun writing it from Maddie's point of view. Researching language and products of the 1800s were both challenging and fascinating.

If there were a real Jose Gasparilla, I would hope that he had some good in him. Maybe he met God one night on that beautiful sea.

Then, of course, Lizzie should have ancestors from her mountains. And who more deserving of attention than the Cherokee? The mountains were theirs, although they made no claim. The Cherokee loved the land and did not want to destroy the beauty and fortune it provided to them for each day's survival. The stories were numerous of Cherokee legends and actual happenings during their ordeal. I hope this fictional account is to your liking.

During my attempts to search through the ancestors of my family, I realized it is difficult to continue going backward when I found a native American in the family tree. The records are sparse and hard to locate if indeed there are any.

Moments – the times that flow are moments in eternity. From generation to generation, we are all related. What fun it will be to one day meet those that have gone before, that have shaped our lives.

-Tricia

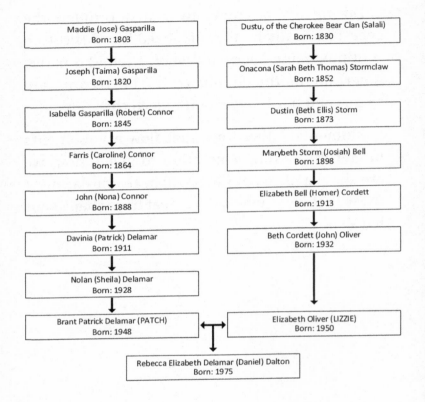

Rebecca, along with her children Elizabeth (Lanie) and Katherine (Katie) continue the family story in *End of Summer*.

Go to www.triciacundiff.com for a free excerpt from the book.

RESOURCES:

What a wonderful world we live in! With all the searches possible on-line and the Limitless Libraries organization through our school systems, doing research has never been more rewarding!

A lot of material was gathered through Wikipedia and Google, but there were also books and other sources that made the research both enjoyable and educational. I have listed below those sources that offered the most valuable material.

Myths of the Cherokee and Sacred Formulas of the Cherokees
by James Mooney

The Cherokee Indians
by Nicole Claro

Trail of Tears: The Rise and Fall of the Cherokee Nation
by John Ehle

Pirates – the Golden Age of Piracy
by Hourly History

The Republic of Pirates
by Colin Woodard

News blurb:

The legend of Jose Gaspar and the history of Gasparilla
by Sarah Phinney/ABC–WFTS Tampa Bay

There are many stories, legends, and myths surrounding Jose Gasparilla/Jose Gaspar. Although the first story I heard about him became the inspiration for this book (on a boat ride around the island by an excellent tour guide), the character should not become one with the legends or myths published before. This book is a work of fiction, and as such, while Gaspar may be a pirate, his character was created to fit into the story's timetable and purely fictional life.

Accounts of Jose Gaspar/Gasparilla note that there is no record of such a man in any documents that would prove his existence. It is left to our imagination to wonder at his life and death.

I like this story the best.

Made in the USA
Monee, IL
23 July 2020